THE
PRODIGAL

CORPSE WHISPERER
THE SERIES

H.R. BOLDWOOD

OLIVERHEBERBOOKS

PRAISE FOR H.R. BOLDWOOD

"If Anita Blake and Stephanie Plum had a lovechild, it would be Allie Nighthawk. One of the funniest and freshest takes on the zombie genre I've read, with genuine heart at the core of the humor and gore."

— DANA FREDSTI, AUTHOR OF THE *ASHLEY PARKER* SERIES AND THE *SPAWN OF LILITH* SERIES

"Anita Blake and October Daye, scoot over to make room for Allie Nighthawk, the fiercest and funniest heroine to hit the streets since Buffy first quipped while laying the undead to rest. *The Corpse Whisperer* is smart, witty, and so much fun you may just start it again as soon as you finish it."

— LISA MORTON, SIX-TIME BRAM STOKER AWARD-WINNING AUTHOR AND CO-EDITOR OF HAUNTED NIGHTS

"The Corpse Whisperer redefines the zombie genre. Allie Nighthawk is the hero we all need more of."

— TOM DEADY, BRAM STOKER AWARD-WINNING AUTHOR

"H.R. Boldwood is the Janet Evanovich of zombie hunters. She's fierce and funny and smart, just like her heroine. She's rejuvenated the zombie genre with her fresh new take, in a kick-ass, take-no-prisoners, balls-to-the-wall series you're going to want to read, time and again."

— CHRISTIANA MILLER, AUTHOR OF
SOMEBODY TELL AUNT TILLIE SHE'S DEAD

CONTENTS

This book is affectionately dedicated to Lisa Morton, friend and mentor, without whose unfailing support and encouragement The Corpse Whisperer series would not exist.

It's also dedicated to my husband Pete, beta reader extraordinaire, as well as Joe, Katie, Tim, Alicia, Isabelle, Ava, and Colette. Love you all to the moon and back.

Last but not least, it's dedicated to the memory of two of Allie Nighthawk's biggest fans:

Rick Burdick who faithfully served as my law enforcement and weaponry expert, and Barbara Kuroff, a wonderfully gifted writer and delightful friend. I wish both of you were here to read the rest of the series as it unfolds. But I know you're up there smiling.

1

———

FLAT BROKE AND BUSTED

Zombie hunting isn't all it's cracked up to be, especially when you're down to forty bucks for gas, a half-pint of Jack, two packs of Ramen Noodles and a freakish skill that comes in handy sometimes — a skill like raising the dead. Most days that's as useful as tits on a bull. But on a good day, I get paid for it.

Corpse whisperers like me don't grow on trees. We don't hang out shingles or advertise BOGO deals or offer 90 days same as cash. Ours is what you'd call a niche market, and frankly, some of us are less diligent than others about putting down the corpses we've raised. That's where the hunting part of zombie hunting comes in handy.

Is this a morbid and occasionally sketchy way to pay the bills? Maybe. But I'm Allie Nighthawk, the best of the badass zombie hunters, and that's how I roll. Unfortunately, after ringing in the New Year, I was also rolling broke.

You'd think that saving the world from deadhead-ageddon would pay well. Think again. I work for myself, subcontracting my talents to local law enforcement agencies. So, when the last moth deserted my wallet, I emptied my bank account and paid

I

for my weapons arsenal to be delivered to a new destination. Shipping munitions costs more than a black market kidney, not to mention there's a shit ton of applicable rules, so I did what any cash poor arms aficionado would do. I hired *Three Men and a Truck* and lied my ass off. I told them they were shipping golf clubs. Lots and lots of golf clubs — and a fifty-gallon drum of something marked 'golf balls.'

Problem solved.

After that, I threw the noodles and my clothes into a duffel, donned my thermal gear, and climbed onto my Harley Lowrider, vowing to make the most of an unexpected warm snap. Then I lit out of St. Louis and headed back to my hometown, Cincinnati.

There were more exciting places on earth, but I owned an empty house there — the house on Pitty Pat Lane that my father had left me when he died three years earlier. The house where I was born some twenty-six years ago. I hadn't been back since Dad's funeral.

Once I hit the outskirts of town, I made a point of scouting out my business prospects beneath the underpasses and railroad trestles, where biters tend to lurk. It was almost midnight — the perfect time for a recon mission since biters come out at night.

Knowing that I'd have a rent-free roof over my head was a great start, but if there weren't enough zombies to wrangle in Cincinnati, I'd be rationing noodles and swiping ketchup packets from street vendors to make tomato soup. I'd seen lean times before, and I could get as creative as the next guy tracking down dinner. But I had limits. Dumpster diving was out of the question. Nobody knows better than a zombie hunter what comes out of dumpsters.

Something caught my eye in the glow of a streetlight. Two uniforms were rousting a skel beneath the Third Street viaduct.

I veered off the exit ramp, stopped about thirty feet away, and turned off my bike to watch the show.

One of the officers caught me from the corner of his eye and waved me off. "Police business, ma'am. Back off, for your own safety."

"Sure thing," I said, not moving a muscle.

The suspect spun toward the sound of my voice. In the yellow glare of the halogen street lights, his face — pale and shadowed with several day's growth — gave off a flat effect. But it was his vacant stare that made me look twice. To an uneducated eye, he could have almost passed for one of the city's homeless.

Almost.

The string of drool that dangled from his lower lip and the tremor in his limbs suggested something else. Well, that and the way he twitched. He didn't shiver. He didn't shudder. He did the full-on undead boogaloo.

Only one thing twitches like that. Freshies — zombies infected within the last seven days. They come across as almost normal except for the whole drooling, twitching thing and the funky, 'south of cheese' smell they give off.

Target acquired, baby.

There were rotters in Over the Rhine. How many remained to be seen. With any luck, I'd be able to afford crackers for my ketchup soup.

Officers TweedleDee and TweedleDum clearly had no idea what they were dealing with. They mollycoddled the meatbag, trying to shoo him down the road like some hapless drifter. A dangerous mistake, expecting a freshie to cooperate — especially a twitcher.

TweedleDee hustled the rotter across the pavement. "Shelterhouse is over on Gest Street, sir. You can sleep it off there. Move along, now."

The biter snarled, bared its teeth and twitched again. This

had ugly written all over it. I climbed off my Harley and planted my feet shoulder-width apart.

"No need to get nasty, sir," TweedleDum said, pulling his taser. "Just move along."

The rotter lunged. TweedleDum fired.

That freshie twitched like frog legs on a hot plate. But it kept coming. After a second useless burst from the officer's taser, I moved in, slipped my Ka-Bar knife from its sheath and plunged it into the brain stem of the biter. Right in the apricot, baby. Bogie down. Then I got arrested and hauled into the 51st Precinct. I hadn't even been in town for ten minutes. A record, even for me.

"Murder?" The word shot from my mouth like a 9mm slug. "Say that again?"

TweedleDum shook his bulbous head. "Where'd I lose you? When you bury a seven-inch blade into a person's head, they call it murder."

Little Allie, the judgmental voice that squats in the back of my brain, took one of her typical cheap shots. *Well, well, well. Look who fell into a steaming pile of shit.*

Freaking brain bitch. Somedays it's all I can do to not scrape her out with a melon baller. I brushed her off with a quiet, "Shut up."

TweedleDee leaned across the table. "You want to repeat that?"

"Look. You've got it all wrong." I said, wiping the perspiration from my forehead. "Your perp was no innocent homeless guy. That thing was a biter."

The Tweedle brothers stared at me slack-jawed, as if I'd explained the calculation of pi. Time stood still. Crickets chirped. Tumbleweeds drifted through the room. I could have bought them both a vowel and they still would have come up empty.

"Rotter? Meatbag? You know...the undead?" A sweat ball rolled off the tip of my nose and plinked against the table. "Oh, for shit's sake. That skel was a fucking zombie!"

They looked at each other and burst out laughing.

I'd like to say I kept my cool. But anyone who knows me would never believe that. I'll admit, it doesn't take much to rile me. But sweet baby Jebus, what a couple of dimwitted douche-nozzles. When I called them that under my breath, they read me my rights and led me down the hallway in cuffs, to a room marked 'Holding.' An electronic buzzer beeped, and the door popped open.

"Wait! Don't I get a phone call? A cigarette...blindfold... anything?" The door slammed behind me. I closed my eyes and listened to the echo of their footsteps fade.

The brain bitch couldn't contain herself. *You screwed the pooch this time. Even you don't look good in prison stripes.*

"Fuck you," I mumbled.

"Oh, I *know* you ain't talking to *me*, bitch."

When I opened my eyes, an Amazon warrior towered over me, with her fist cocked above her head, ready to take me all the way downtown. Our eyes locked. Hers had *crazy bitch* written all over them.

She swung. I ducked and rolled. Her knuckles smashed into the steel door. "Son of a bitch!"

I scuttled across the room, tripping over a third set of feet. After a quick grab at the wall to steady myself, I spun around to find a tiny, prune-faced woman, with gray hair and gunboat feet, seated on a bench along the wall. I darted my eyes back to the Amazon and got my first good look at her. Some things you can't unsee.

She was six-feet at least, wearing a gold lamé bustier with fuchsia hot pants, black fishnet hose and four-inch 'fuck me' red stilettos. Shoulder-length hoop earrings gleamed through her poufy, bottle-blonde hair. A wide swath of dark roots ran along either side of her part, giving her head a weird, reverse skunk stripe.

The Amazon cradled her wounded right hand and tossed me a reluctant nod. "Nice move."

"Helluva punch," I said, staring at the metallic paint chips on her knuckles.

"Fucking A." She opened her fingers with a wince and extended her hand. "Tiffany Swarovski."

Hardcore gangsta girl, this hoochie mama. I glanced at the blossoming bruise on her hand and opted for a friendly tap to her shoulder instead. "Allie Nighthawk. Let's see if we can get you some ice."

Granny Gunboats from the bench joined the klatch. "Alma Rhineheart, ladies." Her high-pitched voice, soft and sweet, floated through the room. "Pleased to make your acquaintance."

I knew why I was there. And given her outfit, you didn't need to be a brain surgeon to figure out why Tiffany Swarovski was there. But Alma had me puzzled. Shoplifting? Unpaid parking tickets? Curiosity got the best of me.

"What're you in for, Alma?"

"Body-packing twenty pounds of herb. Who the hell does a cavity search on an old lady? Dirty bastids."

Tiffany and I exchanged silent glances.

We were an impressive bunch of bitches, if I say so myself. The good, the bad, and the ugly — all in one cell. Although I wouldn't speculate out loud which one of us was which.

Tiffany checked her watch and stomped her foot. "Shit. Hope I get an early bond hearing. Come noon, I gotta meet a client at The Blue Note."

Alma snorted. "Talk about a dump."

"Best be watching what you say, sista." Tiffany circled a

long, curved fingernail at Alma. "You might be old, but that don't make no never mind to me. You bleed like anybody else — maybe more if you taking one of them...anticaligula...anticalugula. One of them pills that makes you bleed like a stuck pig."

Tiffany plopped on the bench beside Alma and kicked off her heels with a sigh. "The Blue Note's not so bad. They got a steady clientele. Long as I'm discreet and don't hustle the customers, the owner lets the interested customers hustle me. The food's good. The service, too. Least it was 'til this week, when the bartender got fired for skimming from the till. There's worse places around."

A buzzer rang and the door popped open.

A paunchy, middle-aged officer stuck his head inside. "Nighthawk? Follow me."

Tiffany snatched her stilettos off the floor, then put her hands on her hips. "How'd she get sprung so quick?"

"Magic," the officer deadpanned.

I pointed to Tiffany's bruised hand. "Can you bring her a bag of ice?"

"In a minute. After I take you to Cap."

I nodded *sayonara* to the ladies and walked out the door, wondering: *Who the hell is Cap? And why does he want to see me?*

2

MY KINGDOM FOR A KETCHUP PACKET

The officer escorted me from the basement holding cells to the first floor. Then he led me through a double row of solid oak desks toward the first office on the right, which bore the nameplate: *Captain Philip Dorsey*. Outside of the office, a sour-faced woman, sporting ruby-red lipstick, wire-rims and a varnished topknot, perched behind her desk like a Kabuki warrior. She looked wily.

I'm always up for a challenge.

The battle axe stood, smoothing the wrinkles from her suit, then opened the door to Captain Dorsey's office and stepped inside to turn on the light.

When I followed her, she spun on her heel, flapped her batwings and shooed me back. "No one is allowed in Captain Dorsey's office without his permission."

Freakin' fussbudget. "You're in his office."

"That's different. I work here. I've been Captain Dorsey's secretary for some twenty-five years." She pointed to a worn, formerly-red vinyl chair by her desk. "Sit. Wait. And be quiet."

Her persnickety tone irritated the snot out of me, but I was tired and had lost interest in annoying her, so I did as I was told. No post-it notes slapped to her computer, no coffee-stained mugs collecting dust, no water rings or scratches on her desk, and no donut crumbs in her keyboard. Downright unsettling for a police precinct.

A barrel-shaped man, fiftyish and chrome-domed, rounded the corner and headed my way. His hawkish eyes narrowed with every step. "Miriam." He nodded toward the shriveled desk Nazi and then disappeared into the Captain's office without so much as a glance at me.

"Ms. Nighthawk is here to see you, sir."

He leaned back through his door and motioned me to follow him. I rose from my chair and walked into his office before Miriam could escort me. She frowned, giving me a sense of accomplishment. I batted my eyes at her and instantly scored our first skirmish a draw.

"Nice to meet you, Nighthawk. Captain Philip Dorsey," he said, pointing to a visitor's chair. "Call me Cap."

Once I sat, he leaned across his desk, elbows planted and fingers steepled beneath his chin. I recognized the body language. He was a man prepared to do battle. But *why*?

"You may be wondering why I called you here."

Cheezus, I hate when people do that. It's like they read the thought bubbles floating over my head.

"The coroner confirmed that the man you knifed in the underpass was a zombie."

"You don't say." I leaned back, expecting an apology. The apology never came.

"Is it true, what they say about you?" he asked.

That depends." I squirmed in my crappy red chair. "What do they say?"

"That you raise the dead."

"Let me guess. You're calling bullshit."

"Not at all. Your reputation precedes you, Ms. Nighthawk. I've studied your cases — read the reports. You've extracted invaluable data from the dead and solved some previously unsolvable cases. I'm impressed."

So, he did know who I was. I cocked my head and stared into his eyes, trying to figure out what he wanted. And why, if the coroner had confirmed my kill, I hadn't simply been released.

"Tell me where you've been," he said. "What you've seen around the country. Are these...these creatures everywhere? Are they breeding? Is their population increasing?"

Breeding? Holy hell. There was a disturbing visual. I didn't even want to know how he thought that worked. "No. They can't breed. They're dead. But the Z-virus is spread through their saliva. I don't know for sure, but I think they might be on the rise."

Maybe I was tired, or maybe I just knew where to look, but lately it did seem like there were more deadheads than usual. When I was a kid, the population seemed stagnant, punctuated by sporadic late night sightings. Zombies were just another bogeyman, dregs from the wrong side of the tracks. The general public, tucked safely in their beds, liked it that way.

I didn't clarify for Cap that when whisperers like me raise the dead, we are, in effect, creating zombies. I put all my risen rotters back down, so the status remains quo. But some others, with my particular set of skills, don't give a rat's ass if there's another biter wandering the earth. For them, it's all about money and power.

Cap hadn't taken his eyes off me. "Where are they concentrated?"

"I don't know where they are. I just got here. It's not like they wear bells around their necks. Your guys are here. Have they seen any patterns to their activity?"

"Our Z-population has been low and fairly static. We've never been able to isolate where they come from. They turn up in abandoned buildings and out of the way places. Usually by the time we stumble across them, they're already in an advanced state of decay."

I shrugged. "That makes Cincinnati the typical host environment for biters."

"How can we keep their population down?"

"There's a scientific field devoted to the study of the virus: Carovescology. Until scientists figure out how the disease works and find a cure, the only thing we can do to keep the Z-population in check is protect ourselves against it."

Cap stared, silent as the sphinx, waiting for me to continue.

"The first step in protecting ourselves is being able to identify a zombie and recognize the stage of its disease process. Sure, when they're shambling around in a state of advanced decay, they're easy to spot. But that biter last night was a freshie. It couldn't have turned more than a day ago. And your officers couldn't distinguish it from a homeless guy."

Cap gave a solemn nod and leaned back in his chair. "Fair enough. But what are they...eating? What are they living on? It's not like we're seeing an increase in missing persons cases."

It's sad that most folks are so preoccupied with their well-fed, middle class lives they haven't figured that out.

"Think about it," I said. "They live in the shadows. They come out at night and eat flesh. What's their obvious food source? The homeless, the addicts, the drifters — people living on the fringe. Let's face it. They're walking-talking fast food for zombies. Lots of those folks are anonymous by choice. Who's going to miss them?"

Cap managed a small, sad smile. "Makes sense, doesn't it?"

He hesitated before he spoke again, as if he had something more to say but wasn't sure if he should.

Finally, he blurted, "I knew your mother, back in the day."

I leaned in closer. "Say that again?"

"Your mother Elena and I were friends. She helped me through a rough patch. Remarkable woman."

I couldn't think of a response, and truthfully, if I had, the lump in my throat would have kept me from spitting it out.

Cap stood to signal our discussion had come to an end. "I have a proposition for you, Nighthawk. I don't need a full-time employee to tackle the few zombie-related crimes we have, but I could use you, from time to time, as a paid consultant. Does that sound like something you'd be interested in?"

'Paid' was all I needed to hear. Although, I'd have preferred benefits and a weekly paycheck. "Are we talking about putting Zs down or raising them? I can tell you right now, raising a corpse costs double."

Cap snorted. "I'm offering you work, and you're shaking me down?"

"Simple mathematics. Every corpse I raise needs to be put back down. Twice the work, twice the money."

"There'd be a few stipulations," he said, as he walked me to the door. "You'll have to keep track of your hours and expenses. And you'll be responsible for your own ride. No cruisers or access to the city's motor pool." He blocked my exit and stared deep into my eyes. "You'll have to carry your own liability coverage, of course."

Apparently, my reputation *had* proceeded me. I didn't have a job. For God's sake, I was living on Ramen noodles and ketchup soup. How the hell was I supposed to pay for liability insurance? Taking down deadheads wasn't always as simple as shoving a knife into a brain stem. On occasion, my services have been known to inflict some...collateral damage. But there are always casualties of war, some in terms of life and some in terms of material goods.

Suck it up, Cap, I thought. *Get ready to pull out your checkbook and don't be skimpy with the zeros.* I reached back to his desk and snagged one of his business cards. "Of course, I have coverage. I'll text you my number."

Little Allie almost swallowed her tongue. *Liar, liar! Pants on fire! Shame! Shame! Shame!*

"Oh, shut your yap," I mumbled.

Cap frowned. "I'm sorry. Did you say something?"

"Just...thank you. And call when you need me."

That stupid brain bitch would be the death of me, yet.

I left Cap's office, winked at Miriam and graced her with a victory grin. But the moment lost its magic when my empty stomach growled like a wounded bear. Miriam scowled and returned to her work.

"Hey," I asked, as I sauntered past her desk. "You wouldn't have any ketchup packets in your drawer?"

I left the precinct thinking about my mother. I supposed it wasn't impossible that she and Cap had been acquainted. They were roughly the same age, and she'd lived here her whole life until she died. I was eleven at the time, and I'd inherited my 'gift' from her. It sucked that I'd lost her before she could teach me how to control it.

For the moment, more pressing matters demanded my attention. I had a roof over my head, and as of today, a new part-time gig consulting with the police. But nothing else had changed. I stopped at Ricardo's Pizzeria, next to the precinct, and wandered inside — ostensibly to use the restroom. On the way out, I filched a handful of ketchup packets from the sidebar. Breakfast awaited. But zombie hunters don't live on condiments alone. I needed food. And money.

I texted Cap my number, then drove through the early morning streets, hoping to be struck by inspiration. Maybe my Lowrider knew where it was going, or maybe I subconsciously chose a route that would take me past The Blue Note Lounge. I remembered my conversation with the hooker in the holding cell. Something about them having an opening for a bartender.

I parked at the curb and walked to the door, fully believing that at this early hour the place would be closed. To my surprise, the door swung open and I was instantly greeted by the stinky ghost of cigarettes past. It was dark inside. My eyes adjusted and found walls that were covered in 1950's wood paneling and flickering neon beer signs. Back-to-back red vinyl booths lined the center of the room. The bar top ran the entire width of the far wall.

A vacuum cleaner droned somewhere out of sight, letting me know I wasn't alone. I ventured in, strolled over to the bar, and ran my hand along its varnished wooden top. It was solid grain, not veneer. Burled walnut. The building was a ramshackle dump, but the bar itself was a thing of beauty. I pictured myself working behind it, and it suited me.

"Sorry, we're closed. Don't open 'til eleven."

I whirled around to find an old fart, seventy if he was a day, with long gray hair and a scraggly beard that swallowed his face whole. Nice eyes though. You can tell a lot about a man by his eyes.

"Hope I didn't startle you," I said. "Word on the street is you're down a bartender."

"That so?" He eyed me cautiously. "Mind telling me where you heard that?"

"One of your patrons. Tiffany..." *What the hell was her name?* "Tiffany Swarovski. I bumped into her yesterday and she happened to mention you might be hiring."

"Could be. Let's sit down and have us a chat."

He motioned me to the closest booth.

The padding whooshed beneath my butt as I slid across the duct-taped vinyl seat.

"You know how to open cans and bottles?"

I grinned enthusiastically.

"Can you spray water and pop out of a tap? Pour the occasional glass of wine?"

"I can handle that." My mind raced. *Please don't ask if I know how to make a Harvey Wallbanger.*

"And what if he does?" the brain bitch screamed. *"How many lies can you tell in one day?"*

Honest to God, sometimes I want to reach inside my head and bitch slap the crap out of that head hag. My stomach rumbled again, loudly reminding me that I hadn't eaten in forever. I closed my eyes and hoped that he hadn't heard it, but there was little doubt.

"Name's Dallas," he said. "Dallas Monroe."

I told him my name and instantly regretted it.

"Well, Allie Cat. If you can show up on time, put your nose to the grindstone, and keep your fingers out of my till, you got yourself a job. Ten bucks an hour. It's only part-time, you understand, but it's better than nothing. Come back around three this afternoon. I'll show you what's what."

Wow. We'd have to work on that nickname.

"Thank you, sir." I stood up to leave and a wave of dizziness washed over me. "You won't regret this." My knees buckled. I grabbed the edge of the table, thinking I was going down. Dallas reached for my arm, but I pulled away. No way I needed some gum-grinder propping me up.

His old, crinkly eyes softened. "There is one thing you could do for me now, if you wouldn't mind. I was about to fix breakfast, eggs, bacon, toast and some hash browns. Care to join me? I hate to eat alone."

3

—————

TURN RIGHT AT THE SOUTH PACIFIC

Dallas produced bottomless skillets of scrambled eggs and even threw some pancakes into the mix. I thanked him profusely, told him I'd be back at three, and headed home, stomach full and spirits high. In town just over a day, I'd already been hauled in for homicide and found two part-time jobs — without even making it to my house. Say what you will. My life is never boring.

I pulled into the driveway, mouthing a silent thank you that I'd remembered to call ahead to have the utilities turned back on. No sooner had I taken my keys from the Harley's ignition, than a ghost from my past charged across the lawn. The blue-haired specter was five-feet-two, weighed close to two hundred pounds, and wore support hose that billowed around her cankles. The ghost's name was Nonnie Nussbaum. She'd lived in the house next door since before I was born.

"Who are you? So noisy, with the *vroom-vroom-vroom*." She glared at my Lowrider. "What your business here?"

"I live here."

"Is lie. No one live here long time."

"I'm Allie, Mrs. Nussbaum. Charlie and Elena's daughter."

She studied me over the top of her wire-rims, lips pursed, a single eyebrow raised. "Where you been all this time?"

"Away." I wasn't about to discuss my life of zombie hunting and raising the dead with a near stranger.

She jutted out her chin. "Why you come back now?"

Nosy old biddy. I shot her my best stink eye (better known as my Allie eye). "I came back because I can, Mrs. Nussbaum. My father died and left me the house."

The tiny fossil harrumphed and threw up her hands. "Welcome home. Watch noise, all that *vroom-vroom-vroom*. And no parties. I like quiet."

She marched back into her house, mumbling in her own bizarre dialect, a mishmash of Yiddish Italian, or was it Italian Yiddish? Twenty seconds later, her hawk-like eyes peered out from between her living room curtains, tracking my every movement.

Flashbacks of living next to Mrs. Nussbaum invaded my brain.

"Please, God," I prayed. "Enough with the memories." But no dice. God has a wicked sense of humor and a very long memory. It wasn't like He owed me.

The house didn't look bad for having stood vacant the last three years. I'd set aside money from my dad's estate to pay for maintenance and lawn care. I opened the front door and a wave of musty air wafted out. January wasn't exactly the time of year to throw open your windows and blow out the stink. I opened them a crack and turned on the exhaust fans. Once I could afford it, I'd buy some Febreze.

The inside was the same as it had been when Dad died. I opened the hall closet and pulled out a set of sheets for my bed. *My* bed. I smiled at the thought. Memories of sweet dreams, snuggling with my mom and feeling safe flooded my mind.

I plopped on the bed and kicked off my shoes, with every intention of putting on the sheets after I rested my eyes for a few minutes. A half-hour later, *Three Men and a Truck* pulled into the driveway with my supply of 'golf clubs.' Twenty-two cartons worth — and a fifty-gallon drum of ~~napalm~~ 'golf balls.' Mrs. Nussbaum, nose smashed against her living room window, surveilled the delivery as if she were on a stakeout.

I'd prepaid to have the guys bring the delivery inside and stack the stuff in my basement and a spare bedroom, where I would lock it up for safe keeping. By the time they finished and drove away, it was nearly two o'clock. I jumped in the shower, changed my clothes, and headed back to The Blue Note.

I walked inside and Dallas met me with a smile. "Son of a bitch. You showed up. And five minutes early, to boot. Let's get started."

He walked me back to his office and showed me where to hang my coat. I took off my duster, and wiggled out of my shoulder holster, giving Dallas an eyeful of my gun.

"You got a concealed carry for that, Allie Cat?"

"Sure do. A girl's got to be careful these days."

No use telling him why I really needed fire power — yet. Maybe later, after he saw how indispensable I was. He'd be less likely to fire me. I slid my seven-inch Ka-Bar knife into the center drawer of his desk.

Dallas whistled. "That's a whole lot of careful for such a little girl. Your weapons stay locked in my office while you're working. Capiche?"

"Sure thing, boss."

He showed me how to stock the bar, ice it down and run the register. He gave me a copy of the price sheet and told me to memorize it. My heart sank when he handed me a bucket and a mop. The barroom floor and rest rooms had to be cleaned twice a day.

I'd mopped the bathroom and was heading out to clean the bar area when Dallas, working a crossword puzzle, asked, "How much for a Bud?"

"Tap, bottle or can?"

"Good girl. Tap."

"Two-seventy-five. A bottle's three-fifty, and a can's three even."

"You're going to work out fine," he said. "Be nice to the customers. Smile. It'll help with the tips. We get hookers here from time to time. You'll know 'em when you see 'em. Long as they don't hassle the customers, I don't care who they leave with or what they do when they're gone. Got it?"

I pictured Tiffany Swarovski and smiled.

Around three-thirty, two guys walked in. Dallas glanced up from his crossword puzzle and filled me in. "The tall one on the left is Jimmy McQueen. Nice enough, 'til he starts in on the whiskey. Don't be afraid to cut him off if you need to. The guy on the right's Hank Bowers. Quiet, keeps to himself. Likely won't say three words to you. He's a regular. Keep his Miller coming and you'll be fine."

Customers drifted in and out, and the hours flew by. Dallas got off his keister when the crowd got thick. I held my own, and I could tell by the way Dallas flashed me a grin or two that I'd exceeded his expectations.

The door opened around eight and in walked Tiffany Swarovski. She took one look at me and stopped in her tracks. "Damn, baby. You working here now? I get a finder's fee or something?"

"You'll get whatever you order," I said. "But no finder's fee. And no free drinks. What brings you by?" As if I didn't know.

She threw me a wink. "Just getting my drink on and looking for some company."

"Well, don't look at me."

She threw back her head and laughed a little too loud. But

it was a good laugh, genuine and warm. "Gotta find somebody," she said. "Had to pay my fine this morning. I need some money, honey."

"Tell me about it."

She sipped a seven-seven and talked my ear off, telling me she was half Polish, half Latina and half Niuean.

I did the math and frowned. "Say what?"

"Well. Numbers aren't my thing." She snagged a handful of bar nuts and flipped them into her mouth, one at a time.

"Polish, Latina, Niuean," I said. "I didn't know that was a thing."

"It's a thing. Head to the South Pacific and turn right. Look for an itty-bitty island."

For all I knew, she was telling the truth. She looked Polynesian, with her caramel complexion and almond-shaped eyes. I liked this chick. She was smart and tough and knew how to take care of herself. We had more in common than either of us might have cared to admit.

Customers began to filter out. Some lonely guy sidled up to Tiffany and made his move. She glanced my way, sat a fiver on the bar top, and left for the night. She didn't have a fiver to spare.

Jimmy and Hank were still throwing 'em back. When I walked behind them to push in a couple of stools, Jimmy reached around and pinched my ass. I turned to sock him into next Tuesday, but Little Allie intervened. *Make nice. He's in here all the time. You need his tips.*

I sucked in a breath and said, "I'd really appreciate it if you didn't do that, Jimmy."

He grabbed my arm in a vice grip as I turned to walk away. "C'mon, baby. Give us some sugar."

Dallas was already out of his seat and on his way over, but nobody fights my battles for me. I grabbed Jimmy's free hand

and bent his fingers back. Not hard enough to break them but enough to hurt.

"Holy crap," he screamed, letting go of my arm. "All right. All right. You win. You don't have to be such a bitch."

Dallas moved alongside me and tried to intervene, but I waved him off and gave Jimmy the Allie eye. "I think you've had enough. Time to go home."

"You can't cut me off, little missy. Only Dallas here can." He looked over my shoulder, hoping for a reprieve. He wasn't going to get it.

I grabbed his hand again, like I was going for round two. "Dallas wasn't serving you. I was. Now, leave. Before I show you what I can do to your balls."

Jimmy hopped down from his stool, scraped his money off the bar, and grumbled as he wobbled toward the door.

"Yo, Jimmy," I called, after he passed the jukebox. "We're not going to do this dance again, are we?"

"No, ma'am," he mumbled, rubbing his fingers.

I realized, as he walked out into the night, that he hadn't left me a tip. That's okay. I'd given him one that he would be smart to remember.

Dallas smiled like a proud papa. "Nicely done, Allie Cat."

Hank Bowers' eyes opened wide. "I know you. You're Charlie Nighthawk's kid. That...that...body snatcher."

And...busted. *Thanks, butt munch.* "It's corpse whisperer."

"Yeah, I've seen you on the news. You're a badass. Drilling zombies and raising the dead. Damn, Dallas. A real celebrity, working here in The Blue Note."

Dallas turned to me in silence.

"That's only for the police and only part-time," I said, struggling for a conversational tone. "When I'm not working here. Which reminds me, I may have to leave early, from time to time, you know, if my...services are required. That's okay, isn't it? I mean, this doesn't change anything?"

Dallas didn't answer.

I swallowed hard and looked him in the eye. "I still have a job, right?"

He rubbed his chin and sighed. "Yeah. You still got a job. You're a damn good barkeep, and you can handle yourself better than any man I ever saw. We'll figure it out."

He glanced at the Budweiser wall clock. It was almost ten-thirty, and the place was deserted. "I think we've had about as much fun for one night as we can stand. Go on home and get some sleep. See you back tomorrow night, eight to midnight."

He counted out seventy-five dollars from the till, for seven and a half hour's work. Then he handed me an extra ten for "putting Jimmy in his place."

I shoved the money into my pocket, along with the thirty I'd collected in tips, and promised to return Friday. The January wind buffeted my face as I steered my Lowrider through the sleepy Cincinnati streets toward home. My phone went off in the pocket of my jeans, surprising the shit out of me. I pulled over to take the call.

"Hello?"

"Ms. Nighthawk? Harry Delk, here. I'm a shield with CPD. We've got a rotter sighting. Meet me at the Third Street viaduct, ASAP."

"*We* have a case, as in you and me? Or we have a case as in I'm helping *you* guys out?"

"Oh." The pregnant pause that followed didn't bode well. "I'm your new partner. Didn't Cap tell you?"

Oh, hell no.

"See you in twenty," I hissed through clenched teeth.

Partner? What partner? Nobody said anything about a partner.

4

———

HEADBUTT

This was the second Zombie sighting at the Third Street viaduct in two days. It was safe to say we'd uncovered a biter hole. I pulled up to the curb cursing under my breath, pissed because I'd been saddled with a partner. The cursing grew louder when I got a load of Harry Delk. No pun intended.

The guy was more round than tall, mid-fifties maybe. His stomach dunlapped his checked, polyester pants and strained against the buttons of his shirt, threatening to launch them at any time. What little hair he had was gray and swept to the side in a comb-over. His eyes looked tiny and trapped behind a pair of thick, black-framed glasses, and his cheeks were covered with a salt and pepper (mostly salt) three-day stubble.

Great. Ancient, nearly blind, and super-sized. Just the kind of partner everyone wants. But to be fair, I don't do partners to begin with. All they do is cause me agita, slow me down and get in the way.

Cap would hear about this.

I climbed off my Harley, sucked in a breath, and counted to ten. It might as well have been four-hundred; I was still going to be pissed when I finished counting.

"Harry Delk," he said, sticking out his pudgy hand.

"Nice to meet you." I strode past him toward the darkened recesses beneath the viaduct. The smell of piss and sweat stung my nose.

Harry called from behind. "A couple of badges called it in about a half-hour ago. Single biter. When they shined a light on the sucker, it shuffled back into the dark."

"Shuffled, you say."

"Shuffling isn't good, is it?"

"No, it's not," I said, wondering how he knew that. "If shuffle is an accurate description of its gait, we need to stay on our toes. Freshies don't shuffle. Neither do flesh-eaters, biters that turned less than a couple of months ago. But corpsicles—"

"Shuffle," Harry said. "They're the seniors of the zombie population. We'll probably smell them before we see them."

What do you know? Harry had done his homework.

"You coming?" I asked, fixing him in the beam of my flashlight. "We're not going to find this thing under a streetlight."

I figured if Tubby couldn't keep up, I'd leave his ass in the dust and handle this myself.

Why is it, every time I make a judgment call, the brain bitch plays armchair quarterback? *Don't you dare leave him behind! He has no clue what he's up against.*

His footfalls faded behind me as I trudged on, silently scolding Little Allie and telling her to take a hike. I peered through the rubble beneath the bridge, shining my flashlight side to side, and up and down. Nothing unusual. Until a shot rang out. I sprinted back and found a corpsicle lying flat on its back, maybe ten yards from Delk, with a perfectly centered hole between its eyes.

"Case closed," Harry said, holstering his .38.

"Did you get lucky or have you been holding out on me?"

"What do you mean?"

"How'd you know to shoot that rotter in the head? Nobody else around here has a clue about wrangling zombies."

"I've worked these streets at night for thirty years. I've seen some shit, let me tell you. Did a little research. Pulled a few strings. That's why I'm working with you now."

"You sandbagged me, Harry."

"Only a little."

A biter lurched from the darkness and grabbed Harry's shoulder. He tried to shake it off, but lost his balance and fell, kicking at the meatbag's face as it inched closer. It opened its jaws and dove for his calf. Lucky for Harry, the only thing that biter had a chance to taste was the lead I fired from Hawk — my custom 9mm, semi-auto Nighthawk.

What else would I carry?

Harry, flat on his back, looked up and nodded. "Nice shot," like we were comparing targets at the range.

I bent down to help him to his feet when a low growl hummed behind me. I spun around and sucked in a breath at the sight of a dog with its teeth clamped onto the leg of another zombie that had shambled onto the scene. If the dog hadn't growled, I'd have never known the biter was coming. The dog held the rotter in place and I took the shot.

That made three corpsicles in one night, plus the freshie from the night before.

After clearing the rest of the viaduct, making sure there weren't other rotters lurking, I returned to Harry, who had scrambled to his feet, rubbing his knee. The dog trotted over and sat beside him, and I got my first good look at the pup. A hefty male bulldog, unbitten, its coat matted with mud and muck. No collar. No tags. And the nails of a gargoyle. The mangy mutt smelled worse than the corpsicles we'd just put down. More than likely a stray.

Take him home, Little Allie whispered. *You owe that dog. He saved your life.*

For the first time in my life, the brain bitch and I agreed on something.

"You okay to walk?" I asked Harry.

"Yeah. Just sore is all. I got more grit than you'd think by looking at me."

"No shit."

"You...ah...you saved my life just now," he said. "I owe you one."

"Forget about it. But...if you really want to thank me, put the dog in your back seat and take him to my house."

"Why would I do that?"

"Because you owe me."

"It's not your dog."

"It's a stray."

"It's dirty and it stinks. You take it home."

"I drive a Harley, Harry. Where am I going to put him? On my lap?"

Harry sighed. "Fine. Whatever. But then we're square. C'mon, boy. Let's follow your new master home."

"No. You do the paperwork for this little soiree, and *then* we're square."

"Anything else?"

"That'll do. For now."

Harry followed me home, got out of his car, and strolled up my sidewalk with the bulldog trailing behind him. When I opened the door, the dog trotted inside like he owned the place.

"Thanks for dropping him off," I said. "Oh, and for doing the paperwork."

"No problem. I can do it in my sleep after all these years. See you next time."

The smartass in me would have told him fat chance, because I didn't need or want a partner. But the hunter in me figured he'd earned a shot.

"Yeah. See you next time."

The good news was that I had $115 dollars in my pocket which I didn't have earlier. The bad news was that I still had the same two packs of noodles and ketchup soup to eat. I fixed it all, thinking I'd go to the store in the morning. Then I fed it to the dog. He needed it more than me.

"Guess I know where my tip money's going," I said, scratching him beneath his chin.

My hand came away filthy, so I filled up the tub and scrubbed him down several times. I wasn't sure that he'd ever had a bath, and was even less sure he enjoyed it, but he endured it without complaint.

I toweled him off, cleaned the tub, and then took my own shower. When I stepped back out of the bathroom, the dog was sound asleep on the kitchen furnace vent, letting the hot air blow against his skin. Smart dog. Strong, too. And loyal. A survivor — like me.

I sat beside him on the floor, brushed my hand against his soft clean fur and whispered. "Thanks for saving me out there tonight. You're a good dog and a kickass zombie hunter. How'd you like to stick around, huh?"

With that, he lurched from the floor to lick my face and accidentally headbutted me.

"That's enough love for one night," I said, rubbing my forehead.

He settled back down on the register and fell asleep. I turned off the lights, lay down on my still bare mattress and pulled a top sheet over me. As I drifted off to sleep, I was struck with a flash of inspiration.

I would name my zombie-hunting dog *Headbutt*.

5

MORE OF A SHUDDER, REALLY

My phone rang at the ungodly hour of 6:00 a.m. Cap asked me to be at the Medical Examiner's office by 8:00 a.m. to raise someone named Veronica Henry, who'd been murdered overnight. Apparently, she had called in to CPD the day before, claiming to have dirt on someone she refused to identify. She had gotten cagey and refused to discuss the specifics over the phone, so CPD scheduled a meeting with her for three this afternoon.

That was one appointment Veronica Henry wouldn't be keeping.

CPD hadn't found any trace evidence at the murder scene, and by the time the body was discovered, any potential witnesses were long gone. Cap had enough stones to call the DA at a quarter 'til five and beg an unscheduled meeting for seven-thirty. Harry would handle the meeting. He'd be requesting a raising order, giving me the right to raise the corpse for investigative purposes. Once he got the order, he'd join me at the ME's office.

That gave me less than two hours to get my ass in gear, shower, dress and grocery shop for the cheapest food capable of sustaining life, both human and dog. I couldn't carry much on my Harley, but it didn't really matter. $115 wouldn't buy a hell of a lot anyway.

I bought my usual staples: peanut butter, bread, Doritos and a big-ass bottle of Jack Daniel's. Headbutt ended up with a red rubber ball, dog treats, and a fifty-pound sack of corn, wheat gluten and meat by-products. In an emergency, we could share.

I arrived at the ME's office fifteen minutes ahead of schedule, ready, willing and able. Harry hadn't arrived yet, so I took a seat in the lobby and waited for him, thinking, "This shouldn't take long."

As is often the case, I was wrong.

8:00 a.m. came and went. By 8:45 a.m. there was still no sign of Harry. I stood and stretched, then wandered over to the window and glanced down at the street hoping to spot Harry's Crown Vic. No such luck. *Damn it, Harry. Hurry up.*

An older, white-bearded guy wearing scrubs emerged from the morgue and stared at me, as if I were a new breed of insect. "Nighthawk?"

"Yes, sir."

"Doctor, actually. Dr. Blanchard. I'm the ME. Where's your raising order?"

"I'm waiting for Harry Delk to bring it."

Blanchard breathed in deeply and exhaled through his nose. "We need to get this show on the road. My drawers are full, and I need the table space."

The ME wasn't a happy man. My phone rang and I yanked it from my pocket, happy for the reprieve. It was Harry, thank God. I signaled Blanchard to hold on and walked outside to take the call.

"Harry, where's our order?"

"We didn't get it."

"What do you mean?"

"The DA refused to take our request to the judge. He said we don't have cause to raise — that she was just another hooker, and hookers get murdered all the time. He mentioned the words 'fishing expedition' and said that, by law, the testimony of the undead is inadmissible as evidence anyway. And that if her family raised a stink, there'd be a ton of bad press. He didn't want any of part of it."

Fucking turdball. Whose side was the DA on, anyway? He knew the law better than I did. If a coroner deemed a raising necessary to prove cause of death, or if law enforcement required a raising for a felony investigation, no permission was required from the next of kin.

I felt the heat rise in my cheeks. "What are our options?"

"We could approach the judge ourselves, but without the DA's support, we'd likely be spitting in the wind."

"What about the Feds?"

"No way. You know what their mantra is? 'It's not under their jurisdiction.'" Harry's tone turned dry. "We can always wait for a new DA."

"Bullshit. This is ridiculous."

The door opened behind me and Doc Blanchard emerged. Apparently, he had been watching through the window.

"What's going on?" he asked.

"The DA won't request our order. Says we're fishing."

It was Doc's turn to go ballistic. "This is a freaking waste of time. I'm the ME, damn it. My duty is to extract all obtainable evidence from a corpse to determine the cause of death. That shouldn't take a fucking act of Congress."

"You know what? You're right," I said, opening the door to the morgue and ushering Doc inside. "Let's do this. Better get here fast, Harry. Things are about to get interesting."

Harry arrived within minutes.

Veronica Henry lay on the ME's table covered by a sheet, her tawny skin and tan lines still visible, even in death. She'd been tall, with endless legs, willowy arms, and long auburn hair. Elegant looking. As a high-priced call girl, those attributes had no doubt served her well.

She'd been stabbed in the back. Rigor was present but not complete, suggesting she'd been dead less than eight hours, give or take. I'm not a medical examiner, but I am a corpse whisperer. I know the stages of death.

When I placed my hands over Veronica's body, Dr. Blanchard got cold feet.

"Ms. Nighthawk, what I stated outside earlier was my opinion. I believe I have the right to approve the raising of a corpse in my capacity as the medical examiner. And if asked that question, I will say so. But *you* do not act under my authority, and I did not instruct you to raise this corpse. Do you understand what I'm saying?"

"I understand what you're trying *not* to say. If asked, you'll testify to your opinion that you can authorize the raising of a corpse. But since you didn't authorize me to raise *this* corpse, I'm screwed, blued and tattooed. Is that about it?"

"Precisely."

Spineless asshat.

I glowered at Doc, then turned my attention to Harry. "Raising can be a little...unpredictable. You ready?"

He stared at my hands poised above Veronica's body. "Ready as I'm going to be."

The moment I closed my eyes, I felt the familiar burning sensation in my palms that signals energy flowing from me into another body. Then I prayed. The prayer wasn't long and it wasn't audible. It was me asking for God's guidance in the use of this awesome, terrible gift He'd given me.

"Veronica, in the name of God, I command you to rise."

Her eyes blinked once. Twice.

"Awaken, Veronica. Awaken." Energy arced from me in a sea of brilliant tendrils.

Her eyes snapped open, and she bolted upright on the table.

Doc Blanchard gasped and stumbled away from the gurney. Harry held his ground, eyes unblinking and fixed on Veronica. She grabbed my hand and squeezed reflexively then darted her eyes around the room.

The dead find the raising process confusing, even terrifying. That's the part I regret most, causing them even more discomfort than they knew at the moment of death. "Veronica, can you hear me?"

"Yes."

"Do you know where you are?"

She glanced around the room again as if analyzing her surroundings, the morgue drawers, the instruments, and the gurneys filled with bodies. Then she peered into my eyes and asked the same question they always ask.

"Am I...*dead*?"

"Yes. I'm afraid you are."

She shivered once. More of a shudder, really. Like the notion of death frightened her.

"Do you know how you died?"

She frowned and squeezed her eyes closed.

"Did you have an accident?"

"No."

"Did someone hurt you?

She opened her eyes and nodded.

"Do you know who hurt you?"

"No. Didn't see."

My heart sank. All this and the woman had no idea who'd murdered her.

Harry jumped in. "Do you know why you were killed?"

"Find book."

Harry and I glanced at each other.

He moved closer and peered into Veronica's eyes. "What book?"

"My book. Find book."

Harry's voice took an edge. "Where is your book?"

"Stretch."

"Focus, Veronica," I said. "Where is your book?"

"Stretch," she repeated.

"Stretch what?" I tossed up my hands and sighed.

"Stretch," she said with a listless shrug. "So tired. Sleep. Need sleep."

Time for a new question: "You called into CPD and said you had dirt on someone. Who was it? And what was the dirt?"

Her eyes grew wide and her lips began to tremble. "No. No, no!"

She pushed me away and tried to get off the table. I held her in check, which freaked her out more. Zombie hunting rule number seven: never agitate a freshie. Things go pear-shaped faster than you can scream, "Run!" Something or someone had scared this girl shitless.

Damn it. We were so close, but we'd gotten all we were going to get. It was time to let her go. I sat behind her on the gurney, put my arm around her waist, and pulled my Ka-Bar from its sheath. "We'll find who did this to you, Veronica. You have my word. I know you're tired. Close your eyes now. Go to sleep."

I slid the knife into her brain stem, quick and easy. When she collapsed back against me, I slid out from beneath her and laid her shoulders back on the gurney.

Doc bowed his head. Hard-ass Harry wiped his eyes. I swallowed my feelings and strolled to the sink to wash off my knife. No one said this was easy. I just wish she'd seen her killer.

Harry and I headed over to Cap's office to deliver the bad news. Although Cap was concerned about the lack of information Veronica provided, he was more concerned with a procedural hiccup.

"You did *what*?"

"We didn't get the court order but I raised her anyway."

"You didn't have an order?"

Cap's face turned a shade of magenta I'd never seen before. "Why the hell didn't you stop her, Harry?"

"Don't look at Harry. It was my call," I said. "You wanted me to raise her, so I raised her. End of story."

"He was supposed to get the order first and *then* you were supposed to raise her."

"But he couldn't get the order."

Cap rubbed his face with his hands. "You're missing the point. Do you have any idea what kind of a shit storm you could find yourself in?"

Obviously, Cap didn't know me very well. I live in a swirling vortex of shit. It comes with the territory. If I worried every time I ruffled someone's feathers, or broke a rule to get what I needed, I'd never accomplish anything.

"You should be thanking me," I said in a haughtier tone than I'd intended. "Maybe Veronica couldn't tell us who killed her, but she gave us something. She mentioned a book. We just have to find it. And by the way," I reached into my pocket and pulled out a handwritten invoice. "Here's my bill for the other night."

Cap ripped it from my hand and glared at it. "Other than today's, I've only given you one assignment. You've billed me for two here."

"Two biters, Cap."

"Harry killed one of them."

"There were three. He killed one, I killed two. Pay up."

Cap scribbled his initials at the top of the bill and tossed it in his outbox.

My stomach rumbled. "Anything you could do to expedite that would be appreciated."

"I'll get right on it."

Cap could be a dry son of a bitch, sometimes.

"If we're done here," Harry said, getting to his feet. "I've got some background work to do."

"Oh, we're done." Cap eyeballed me, so I took one last shot.

"If it would be easier, I could just add my charges for the raising today to the bottom of that invoice. They'd only have to cut one check. And since it was a raising, I get paid double. Up and down, remember?"

"Goodbye, Nighthawk."

6

WHO'S GOING TO MOP THE FLOOR?

Harry and I walked out of Cap's office together. He had the investigative piece of Veronica's murder to work on, and I had plans of my own. We'd found one biter hole, but surely there were others.

"Other than the Third Street viaduct, where in town would I likely find some zombie nests?"

Harry ran his hand across his comb-over and paused. "First place I'd tell you to look would be the abandoned subway tunnels. Next, I'd try the old Hudepohl Brewery building off Interstate 75. Then, maybe The Crosley Building on Arlington Street."

We turned to go our separate ways, and Harry called back over his shoulder. "Shout if you need me."

The guy knew his stuff, and he wasn't half bad company. *What the hell?*

"Hey, Harry. I work part-time at this dive called The Blue Note. Over on Liberty. I'll be there tonight from eight to twelve. Stop by if you get bored."

His face lit up. "Dallas's place? I know it well. I'm in there more than nights than I should be. Sure. I'll stop by."

I climbed on my Lowrider and headed for Camp Washington to check out The Crosley Building. I'd whizzed past it at seventy miles per hour on the way into town, but I couldn't say I'd noticed it.

I pulled to the curb a couple of blocks back on Arlington and took in the view. The building was massive, eight stories tall, and sprawled for hundreds of thousands of square feet. Most of the façade had broken away and lay beside it on the ground, along with endless amounts of broken glass and crumbling brick.

What impressed me most was its potential to hold an army of biters. Deserted, isolated, and unwelcoming. The perfect place for a nest. I sniffed the air and got a whiff of decay. Harry's instincts had been right. The other buildings nearby were in similar condition and no doubt had their own smaller dens of deadheads.

I made a mental note to check with Cap. Maybe he could find out if The Crosley, or any of the surrounding properties, were scheduled to be razed. If they weren't already on the list, I'd recommend they be added. Of course, when that time came, we'd either have to go in guns blazing, or develop a tactical plan to waste the rotters as they scurried out of their hidey-holes and onto the streets, like a multitude of cockroaches. Public relations-wise, a surprise attack in the dead of night, while the city slept, would play better.

The subway tunnels and the Hudepohl Brewery would have to wait for another day. It was a beautiful, crisp afternoon, and I knew where I wanted to go next.

I slowed my Harley to a crawl as I passed through the gate at Spring Grove Cemetery. It had been a while since I'd been there. Three years to be exact. The day I buried my father. The grounds were gorgeous and peaceful, just as I remembered them.

My parents' graves were north of the Dexter Mausoleum,

near a small grove of trees. I sat beside their headstones and chatted with them as though they could hear me, filling them in on my life and how I'd stuck to the rules they'd taught me. At least, for the most part. They would have been proud. Especially my mother.

My stomach growled. I'd missed lunch by several hours, and I needed to check on Headbutt before I started my shift at The Blue Note anyway, so I left, promising my parents to return so we could finish our one-sided chat.

By the time I pulled into my driveway, it was nearly five o'clock. I opened the kitchen door and Headbutt raced past me into the backyard. His bathroom schedule hadn't been uppermost in my mind. I'd have to rectify that. Owning a pet was new to me. At least he hadn't left me any puddles or piles to clean up.

I tore into a bag of Doritos and eyed the bottle of Jack with lust in my heart, but decided against it. I had to be at work by eight. Besides, with any luck, Dallas might slide me a few freebies on the side.

My whiskey ruminations were interrupted by Nonnie Nussbaum's voice filtering through the door. "Stop that! Naughty golem. I get you with broom. Shoo. Shoo."

I peeked through the curtain and moaned. Headbutt stood at the fence line, hiking his leg and squirting pee through the chain link onto Nonnie's rose bushes.

"*I get you*," Nonnie screamed as she flew from her porch, broom in hand, and zeroed in on Headbutt. Apparently, he didn't care for her any more than I did. He barked nonstop until I sprinted outside to the porch. Nonnie glared at me over the top of the fence.

"When you get big ugly dog?"

"Just last night. I—"

"It pee on my roses."

"Sorry," I said, although I truly didn't give a rat's ass. "C'mere, Headbutt. Here, boy. *Here.*"

I clapped my hands.

He ignored my command, turned from the fence and drifted aimlessly through the yard, sniffing everything he passed before plodding back to the porch. The look in his eye said, "I didn't come back because you called me; I came because there's food inside."

Mrs. Nussbaum wrinkled her nose. "Head...*butt*? What kind name that?"

"*His* name," I said with a forced smile. "Let's go inside, boy."

I opened the door and Headbutt trotted inside, earning himself a Dorito — partly because he did as I asked, but mostly because he was a rabble-rousing rule breaker like me. I knew there was something special about Headbutt the moment I laid eyes on him. Well, that and the fact that he knew how to handle a rotter.

He and I spent some bonding time in front of the TV watching The Westminster Dog Show. I scratched his belly and shared a few more of my Doritos with him. I even made fun of the micro, mini, teacup floofy-haired bitches so he wouldn't get a fat dog complex. Somewhere along the line we both took a nap. When I got up to leave for my shift at the bar, he fixed me in his sad bulldog gaze, triggering an instantaneous guilt trip.

I promised him that I'd be back as soon as my shift was over. He lay on the register vent, a dog beholden to no man, closed his eyes, and dismissed me.

Damned, if I didn't like that dog.

The Blue Note was packed to the rafters when I walked in at a quarter 'til eight. I reached for the mop, but Dallas shook his head.

"I need you behind the bar. You can clean later when things slow down."

We worked together like a well-oiled machine, pouring, mixing and popping tops. I washed more glasses that night than I'd washed in my entire life.

Along about ten, Dallas poured a double shot of Jack and slid it over to me. "Think of it as a tip."

My favorite kind of tip, after money. And I was raking in the bucks that night, busy as it was. If this kept up, Headbutt and I might be eating spam once in a while.

Around ten-thirty, Harry walked in the door looking rode hard and put away wet. Dallas, busy packing beer tubs with ice, looked up and threw him a quick wave.

"What you having?" I asked.

He slumped onto a bar stool and sighed. "Surprise me."

I brought him back a Guinness and a shot of Crown. "On the house."

"A boilermaker? Haven't had one of these in years. Don't mind if I do."

He dropped the shot glass into the beer and tossed it back. A real pro, but then, most cops are, in my experience. Hell, I'm not judging. I'm right there with them. Me and Jack Daniels.

For the first time that night, the crowd began to thin. My other customers were still nursing their drinks, so I poured Harry another Guinness, then leaned across the bar and took a well-deserved break.

"Tell me about the real Harry Delk," I said. "Wife? Kids? Batshit crazy mistress who ties you to the bed with scarves?"

Harry spit a mouthful of Guinness down his shirt and laughed. "No to all three. Kind of a workaholic."

He threw back some peanuts and wiped the Guinness off his shirt.

I considered setting him up with Tiffany but talk about an

odd couple. It took all I had to squelch my grin. Not ten minutes later, Tiffany showed up.

She made a beeline for Harry and held out her wrists. "Okay, Officer. Slap on the cuffs. Let's get this over with."

Harry snickered and crossed his arms. "I haven't arrested you since I made detective. Give one of the other cops a chance."

"Really," I said, raising my brow. "You two know each other?"

Tiffany winked. "Harry and me go way back, don't we?"

"As far back as your arrest record, anyway."

"How 'bout buying your favorite working girl a seven-seven? For old time's sake."

He chuckled and pulled a five from his pocket. "Nighthawk, bring the lady a drink."

I served her up and she wandered away, with a final wink at Harry.

"Now, I'm gonna do my thing over there." She pointed to an empty stool beside a lonely looking guy. "Just pretend you don't see me."

"See who?" Harry smiled as she strutted away, shaking her money-maker like a maraca.

He turned to me, rolled his eyes, and changed the subject.

"I got to see you in action today. A little unsettling, but highly impressive, by the way. How 'bout I pick you up tomorrow morning, say nine o'clock? We can poke around the murder scene, ask a few questions — maybe find the book Veronica was talking about. I'll show you how a fat-assed dinosaur cop runs an investigation. Two to one, I find something the officers on the scene missed."

"Two to one? I'll take those odds. You got a deal."

The door burst open, bringing our conversation to a halt. Two uniforms, grim-faced and eagle-eyed, marched across the floor. Clearly, they hadn't come for beer and pretzels.

Dallas cut them off at the pass. "Can I help you, officers?"

"We're looking for Allie Nighthawk."

Harry glanced at me.

I looked at him.

Dallas didn't flinch. "May I ask what for?"

"Police business, sir."

One of the uniforms kept his eyes on Dallas, while the other officer strolled around the room, checking out the patrons. I leaned a little to my left, hoping Harry's big-ass comb-over would block me.

It didn't.

"Allie Nighthawk," the officer said, as he pulled the bracelets from his utility belt and cuffed me behind my back. "You're under arrest."

"What the hell for?" I asked.

"Gross abuse of a corpse."

"Say *what*?"

Cap's aforementioned shit storm had arrived. A category five, from the look of things.

And Little Allie couldn't resist the urge to beat me over the head with it. *How do you do it? Every time I think you can't top yourself, you do. Truly outstanding.*

The words, "Bite me, bitch," tumbled out of my mouth before I could shove them back in.

Harry winced and turned away.

Dallas shot me the stink eye.

The bar patrons gawked and mumbled among themselves.

"That wasn't meant for you," I said, as the officer pulled me across the floor. "This is all a big misunderstanding."

I don't know why I bothered. That line never works for anyone.

"Better you than me, baby," Tiffany hollered. "Need a bail bondsman?"

"Don't worry," Harry called. "I'll tell Cap and get you counsel."

Fuck fuck fuckity fuck. I had a big ol' plate of *I told you so* coming my way. "Harry," I said, straining against the cuffs. "Whoever you get better come cheap. I can't afford toothpaste, let alone an attorney."

The officer dragged me toward the door, and I suddenly remembered Headbutt.

"Harry, can you let my dog out tonight? Please? And maybe stop by in the morning to feed him? The back door's open." Nothing like announcing to the world that your door's unlocked.

Harry's eyes twinkled as he waved goodbye, "Will do. Guess we're off for tomorrow morning, huh?"

I dug in my heels at the doorway and spun toward Dallas. "I promise I'll get this straightened out. Please don't fire me."

As the door swung closed behind me, I heard him say, "Crap. I'm back to mopping the damn floors."

7

———

OPIE DOES BATTLE

freckle-faced boy sat across the table from me in The Hamilton County Detention Center. He was red-haired and skinny. His brown suit hung on him as though it might have belonged to his father. A cream-colored shirt muted his already pale complexion, and his tie, a tan-striped relic from the disco era, boasted more stains than stripes.

He smiled and reached his fish-bellied hand across the table. "Hi. Timothy Andrews, your attorney. Harry sent me."

The brain bitch took one look at him and guffawed. *You are so screwed.*

"You're scheduled to be arraigned at nine," Opie said, frowning at his watch. "We've got twenty-three minutes. Let's discuss why you're here."

"Look, Opie. I'm in real trouble. How 'bout sending your daddy in here."

Opie's emerald eyes narrowed. "Ms. Nighthawk, I suggest you lose the sarcasm and focus on the matter at hand. Your future is at stake. Shall we start again?"

If nothing else, the kid had spunk.

I leaned back in my chair and regarded him in a new light. "Okay, Opie—"

He snapped his briefcase closed and glared at me. "I've read your file, Ms. Nighthawk. And I'm about five minutes younger than you. Call me Opie again, and you can find yourself another attorney. You're wasting time. Your hearing starts in twenty-one minutes."

Little Allie snapped off my bitch-switch without my permission. In hindsight, that was probably a good move. He was my only shot, so I sat up straight and gave him the highlights.

"I raised a female corpse — a hooker and potential informant — to obtain information relevant to the investigation of her murder. Captain Dorsey at the 51st precinct requested my services, subject to the issuance of a court order. My partner presented a request for the order to the DA, who subsequently refused to present it to the judge."

Opie squished his brows together. "Why?"

"Craig Farragut, the DA, said we were fishing — that it wouldn't matter what the corpse testified to because the testimony of the undead isn't admissible in court."

Opie folded his hands on his briefcase and stared into my eyes. "If you didn't have the court order, why did you go through with the raising?"

I squirmed in my chair, and for the first time, pondered that question myself. "The ME, Doc Blanchard, got pissed. He had a full house, and no open autopsy tables. By dicking around, trying to get this order, we were wasting his time. Then he said that he was the ME, and he should be able to examine a corpse in any way he saw fit to determine cause of death."

"And?"

"I went with it. I thought he was right."

We were interrupted by a knock at the door. It was Harry. I told Opie to let him in. The more the merrier.

"You're being charged with gross abuse of a corpse," Harry said. "Do you know what that means?"

"Well, *duh*," I said, rolling my eyes. "If raising her from the grave wasn't freaky enough, maybe it was drilling her corpse in the brain stem with my seven-inch knife."

Harry covered his face with his hands but didn't intervene.

Opie sighed. "It's the word *gross* that concerns me. That's makes your alleged offense a fifth-degree felony."

Sweet Fucking Lorraine! A felony?

To be honest, that could have been my thought, or it might have been the brain bitch's. Hard to tell. We were both stunned.

Opie looked at his watch. "I need to make a quick phone call. Then we'll have to go."

"Go where?"

"Across the street to the court house."

Opie left the room to make his call. When he returned, Harry pulled some strings and got permission to provide me with a private escort to the courthouse, as opposed to me joining the chain gang of losers who would enter through the underground tunnel. Opie accompanied us, wearing a taut smile and a far away look in his eyes. I hoped he was formulating my defense, assuming he thought I had one. Me? I pictured myself in a gray-green jumpsuit and winced. Nobody looked good in those moldy-colored potato sacks.

We sat on a bench outside Hearing Room A and waited for our case to be called.

Opie scribbled some last minute notes in his legal pad. "We've got Judge Franklin today."

"Is that good or bad?" I asked.

"He's a straight shooter. Doesn't go for grandstanding. It could be worse."

When my case was called, we pushed through the double doors and moved to the defense table.

Opie nodded toward a short chubby guy seated across from us. "That's Jerry Milligan, one of the DA's grunts."

Jerry shuffled his papers, dropped his pen on the floor, and banged his head on the table picking it up.

"Please, God," I prayed. "Let him be a doofus."

The clerk of courts rose and announced my case. "The State of Ohio versus Allie Nighthawk."

The brain bitch snickered in my ear. *You're going down so hard!*

Judge Franklin peered over his bench, in our general direction. "Are all parties present?"

Opie and Jerry answered in unison, "Yes, Your Honor."

The clerk gave a formal reading of the charges. "Ms. Nighthawk, you are charged with violation of O.R.C. 2927.01, subsection B, gross abuse of a corpse: 'No person, except as authorized by law, shall treat a human corpse in a way that would outrage reasonable community sensibilities.' How do you plead?"

I leaned into the microphone, cleared my throat, and answered, "Not guilty, as in absolutely no way under the sun would I ever do that. Totally innocent — like a baby lamb, or one of those cute little mini-goats. Your Highness...Honor. Sir."

Judge Franklin glared first at me and then at Opie, who placed his hand over the mic and whispered, "Chill."

It was time for Freckle-Face Strawberry to do his thing.

"Your Honor, the charges in this case are completely without merit. We request immediate dismissal."

Milligan's jaw dropped. "Without merit? She plunged a seven-inch knife into the skull of a corpse!"

"Mr. Andrews," the judge boomed. "This is an arraignment, not a preliminary hearing. We won't be arguing the merits. Let's move on to bail, shall we?"

Milligan glanced across the table at me and squared his shoulders. "Your Honor, the State deems Ms. Nighthawk, having only been in residence here for a grand total of...three days, to be a potential flight risk. We request maximum bail."

Opie rolled his eyes. "Ms. Nighthawk has no criminal record. She owns her own home here in town and has a job consulting with CPD on paranormal-related cases. She isn't going anywhere, Your Honor. We request OR bond."

Judge Franklin banged his gavel. "So be it. Ms. Nighthawk, you are hereby released on your own recognizance. Mr. Andrews, you can confirm the time and date of the preliminary hearing with the clerk before you leave today."

"What?" I asked, grabbing Opie's arm. "We have to come back *again*?"

"I'm afraid so."

"Are you freaking kidding me? Can't you just make this go away?"

"That's the plan," Opie said, nudging me down the aisle toward the hall.

Harry nodded at me from the doorway. "I've got to get back to work. I'll check in with you later."

"Thanks for...everything," I said, feeling a little awkward.

Harry nodded at Opie and grinned. "Thanks for coming down, Tim."

"No problem."

Harry's eyes sparkled when he shifted his gaze to me. "You should probably add Tim's number to your contacts. I have a feeling it'll come in handy."

So far, Harry had saved my ass twice. I could have done far worse drawing a partner. After Opie and I said goodbye to Harry, Opie steered me down the corridor to check on our hearing date. I suppose I should have been satisfied, being out on OR, but all I could see were dollar signs.

"First, an arraignment and now a hearing. What's next?" I asked. "Talk about a freaking racket. You attorneys. You're all a bunch of shysters. I hope you like cornmeal and meat by-products, 'cause that's all I've got to pay you with."

Opie stopped in his tracks. "I told Harry I'd take your case pro bono, but I may have to rethink that. Cheese and crackers, you're high maintenance."

Well, that was pretty damn presumptuous of him, given that he hadn't even scratched the surface.

8

NEWS FLASH

Opie led me down the courthouse steps. I wasn't a happy camper, and I didn't care who knew it.

"January sixteenth? That's ten days off. What the hell am I supposed to do for ten days?"

Opie shrugged and loosened his food-stained tie. "Keep your nose clean and don't raise any corpses without an order until we get this sorted out."

A Channel 10 news van screeched to a halt at the curb, and its crew sprinted up the steps in front of us. A cameraman jockeyed for position and hoisted his camera to his shoulder, then a short, dark-haired woman shoved a microphone in my face and peppered me with questions.

"Ms. Nighthawk, Jade Chen, Channel Ten news. Is it true that you reanimated a corpse without a court order and then killed it by stabbing it in the brain?"

Moron.

"You can't kill a corpse, lady. It's already dead." I pushed the microphone away. "Back off, Buttercup."

"The ACLU has publicly denounced your practice of raising

the dead as a human rights violation. Would you care to comment on that?"

Opie stepped in front of me, shielding me from the camera. "No comment. Let us through please."

Jade Chen swung the mic toward Opie. "Your name, sir? And your affiliation with this case?"

"Timothy Andrews, Ms. Nighthawk's attorney." He grabbed my arm and then bulldozed through the press. "Let us through. Please."

The feisty reporter stood her ground. "Mr. Andrews, what will be your defense? Are you concerned about the public outcry against the practice of raising?"

"No comment. Move out of our way, Ms. Chen, or I'll have you charged with harassment."

"Talk to me, Mr. Andrews. Is there more to this story than meets the eye?"

Opie spun on his heel and turned pitbull. "Other than my client being ambushed here on the courthouse steps? Or you sensationalizing this case for the sake of ratings — casting judgment on my client before her case has even gone to trial? You tell me, Ms. Chen. That's what I see."

"Cut," Jade snapped. "We're finished here." She turned to me with a thin, predatory smile. "We'll get our story, Ms. Nighthawk. With or without your cooperation. Better for you *with*, don't you agree? Think about it," she said, shoving her business card at me. "In case you change your mind."

I slapped the card from her hand and leaned in close. "Careful, Ms. Chen. I bite."

"Was that a threat?"

"No, it was—"

Opie yanked me down the steps and pulled me through the last of the news crew, still packing up their equipment. Once we were out of earshot, Opie stopped short, spun me around and read me the riot act.

"Have you ever considered getting a muzzle for that brass-balls mouth of yours? You can't threaten people, Ms. Nighthawk. Especially news reporters. Don't make my job harder than it is."

After I promised that I'd be a good little corpse whisperer, Opie dropped me off at The Blue Note so I could pick up my Harley. I considered going inside to talk to Dallas and make sure I still had a job, but I decided it might be best to give him some space. Besides, I was tired and Headbutt was probably wondering if I'd abandoned him.

My plan was to get some much needed sleep, and then report to the bar around seven-thirty, hoping to start back to work. With any luck, it would be busy and I wouldn't have to grovel.

I slowed down as I pulled into my driveway, selfishly praying that Mrs. Nussbaum had gone deaf overnight and wouldn't hear my Harley. Fat chance. Prayers like that never work.

The blue-haired fossil scurried out her door and crossed the lawn. "Mrs. Nighthawk," she shouted. "You must *vroom-vroom* more quietly. You wake the dead."

She had no idea how right she was about that. Why she called me Mrs. Nighthawk, I'll never know. Crazy old bat. The odds against me putting up with a husband were astronomical — and vice-versa.

I waved at her, wondering if I would have to start walking my Lowrider down the street and into the driveway. "Yes, Mrs. Nussbaum. You bet," I hollered over my shoulder and sprinted for the door, hoping to avoid a conversation. My bed and a lonely dog called.

After slipping in the key, I turned the knob and rushed in. Headbutt was right where I'd left him, lying on top of the register vent. I was beginning to wonder if he was kinetically challenged. His food bowl was empty and his water dish looked low, so I topped them off and then opened the kitchen door to let him outside. The red ball I'd bought him stared at me accusingly from the kitchen sink. I picked it up and joined Headbutt in the backyard.

Once he'd done his business, he sat in the grass with his eyes glued to me. I showed him the ball, hoping for a reaction. Nothing. Not even a tail wag.

"Fetch?" I said, throwing the ball.

Headbutt watched it sail by, then turned his head and fixed me in his bloodshot gaze.

"Go get the ball! Go on! Go get the ball, boy!"

He yawned and then farted. His stubborn bulldog butt never moved.

"Run, run, run." I trotted toward the ball, hoping he'd take the hint.

He lay in the grass, closed his eyes and ignored me. That dog had no intention of chasing a ball, and probably never would. I picked up the ball, then walked over beside him and bent down.

"That's okay, Headbutt. You do *you*," I muttered, scratching behind his ears.

He gave me a kiss and followed me back into the house, breaking wind the whole way.

My dog. I think I'll keep him.

I finally finished making my bed for the first time since I'd arrived, stripped off my clothes, and then crawled under the covers. Headbutt launched himself up and burrowed in alongside me. Best. Nap. Ever.

I might have slept the night away but Harry called, wondering if I'd be at The Blue Note.

"At least for a few minutes," I said. "Maybe longer if I'm not fired."

Come seven-thirty, feeling like an absolute dillweed, I walked my Lowrider to the street, kickstarted it, and headed for the bar. I practiced my speech for Dallas along the way. But the truth is, from one moment to the next, I never know what's going to come out of my mouth. It's always a crapshoot.

I pulled into the parking lot of The Blue Note and breathed a bit easier. Dallas had a packed house. He wouldn't have the time, or the desire, to rip me a new one. The juke box was blaring and the crowd was in high gear. I spied Dallas behind the bar and sucked in a breath. It was time to throw myself on my sword.

Dallas glanced up and caught my eye. He must have been a good poker player; his expression was tough to read.

"Busy tonight," I said, feeling my cheeks burn. I shifted my weight from foot to foot and finally blurted, "Listen. About last night. I'm sorry. It was all a big misunderstanding."

"A misunderstanding," he repeated. "Let's see, now. Would that be the part where you got arrested for abusing a corpse? Or the part where you forgot to mention that you already had a night job when you accepted this job? Did it ever occur to you that hunting zombies at night might pose a scheduling problem here?"

My freeloading brain bitch pitched a hissy. *Commence groveling. Look pathetic. NOW, Dumbass.*

"I need this job, Dallas. I'm broke. CPD hasn't paid me yet for the couple of jobs I've done. I promise, if you let me work the eight to midnight shift, I'll talk to Harry about scheduling our jobs in the off hours. Sure, there could be some overlap," I said, ignoring Little Allie's screams. "But if, and when, that happens, I'll make it up. Take other shifts. Clean grease traps. Haul out the trash. Bust heads—"

"Just shut up and get back here," Dallas said, pointing toward the ladies' room. "Grab the plunger out of the back and unclog that toilet."

What can I say? The life of a broke-ass zombie hunter isn't always sunshine and roses. Sometimes, you have to deal with shit. Literally.

Around nine o'clock, Harry walked in and bellied up to the bar with Opie.

"ID, please?" I said to my freckle-faced lawyer.

"Your whimsical sense of humor never disappoints, Ms. Nighthawk."

"Just Nighthawk, Opie."

"I'm Tim. Seriously. Is there no end to your abuse?"

"Not really," I said, "I'm a bottomless pit of contempt. Ask anyone."

Harry reached for a fistful of peanuts. "If we're counting, and believe me, I am, I've pulled your fat from the fire twice now. Just curious. Do you get arrested often?"

"More than you'd think," I said, sliding him his Guinness.

"I should have warned you about Jade Chen," he said. "She's direct and very persistent."

Opie's freckles blushed. "She sure is hot."

"She's a bitch," I said, slamming down his can of Bud.

People kept coming through the doors. I ended up waiting tables and taking food orders, not that I knew what I was doing. The only thing I knew for sure was that I wouldn't be the person doing the cooking. Although the patrons had no idea why, they should have been thanking me for that.

Dallas cooked and I tended bar, scrambling around like a one-legged cat in an ass-kicking contest. I checked on Harry and Opie, and brought them another round. Forty-five minutes later, I brought them their third round. Shortly before eleven, the crowd thinned out.

Dallas slid me a double Jack on the rocks and told me to

take a break. I joined Harry and Opie at the bar and relaxed for the first time that evening. I closed my eyes and tuned out the world, until Harry grabbed the TV remote and cranked up the volume. When I opened my eyes, Jade Chen's face stared back at me from the big screen TV mounted above the bar.

Hadn't I been abused enough for one day?

"Good evening, Cincinnati. I'm Jade Chen. The following film clip, shot earlier today on the steps of the Hamilton County Courthouse, relates to charges of gross abuse of a corpse against noted zombie wrangler, Allie Nighthawk."

I covered my eyes, watching the video through splayed fingers and listened for the words I knew were coming: "Back off, Buttercup."

I moaned and banged my head against the bar. Opie the optimist observed that at least the camera hadn't been rolling when I more or less promised to bite her. But bless her cold, black heart, she wasn't finished with me yet.

"The ACLU is digging in their heels on this issue, folks. It appears that dead lives *do* matter. Corpse Whisperer? Or Cadaver Diver? We'll be sure to keep you updated on this case as events unfold. This is Jade Chen, Channel Ten news. May I never appear on your doorstep, microphone in hand, searching for the truth. Goodnight, Cincinnati."

That freaking biatch.

Dallas snapped his head in my direction and I realized, once again, that words meant to float over my head in tiny thought bubbles had actually escaped my mouth.

Dallas simply shrugged and slid another double down the bar.

Good man, that Dallas.

Harry pointed to the screen. "Look — there's Farragut, your favorite District Attorney. He's running for office again."

I flipped Farragut the bird as I listened to his commercial. He boasted that he was tough on crime and spouted his prosecutorial statistics. He even bragged about his stint in the armed forces which, given the picture that popped up, could have been as far back as the French and Indian War. The commercial ended with: "I'm Craig Farragut. And I approve this message."

Harry tossed back his drink and chuckled. "I've seen that ad a dozen times now. This is the first time I ever really listened to it."

"Ugh," I said, flicking him with the bar towel. "Turn that bozo off."

He changed the channel and shot me an evil grin. "You know, I would have been checking out the Henry murder scene this morning, if I hadn't been taking care of your dog and escorting you to court from the slammer. Oh, that's right. You were supposed to be there with me. Shall we try again tomorrow?"

"Wouldn't miss it."

"Allie Cat," barked Dallas. "Clean up in the men's room. Bring the plunger and a mop."

Opie snorted. "Allie Cat?"

"Forget you heard that," I said with a sigh. "He's the only person who gets to call me that — and only until I can break him of the habit."

Harry put money on the bar to cover his tab and got up to leave. I scooped up the cash, noting that he'd left a generous tip.

"Thanks for everything. Seven thirty, tomorrow morning," I said, as he walked away.

I grabbed my tools from the back and walked into the men's room. A trail of vomit stretched from in front of the sink all the way to the john. I hadn't even looked into the toilet yet to see why I needed the plunger.

Little Allie told me: *"Look on the bright side. Sure, you're mopping up somebody else's puke, and so what if there's a meatloaf-*

sized turd wedged in the john. Those things don't matter. You have a job, and you're getting paid for your efforts." **She even said,** *"It could be worse. You could be in jail, scrubbing up the same kind of mess with a toothbrush."*

Sometimes, I want to gouge that bitch out of my brain with a spork.

9

____

DAMN YOU, HARRY DELK

The following morning, Harry picked me up at 7:30 on the dot. When I let him in the door, Headbutt rammed his squat little body into Harry's legs, nearly bowling him over. Harry took it in stride. He even picked up the red ball from the sink, where I'd left it, and rolled it across floor. Headbutt turned his back and sauntered to his favorite register vent, where he plopped down with the density of a fifty-pound sack of potatoes.

"Not into fetch, huh?" Harry asked.

"He's kinetically challenged." Harry's eyebrow raised, so I clarified my diagnosis. "He's a lump of lard with no interest in unnecessary movement."

After Harry and I said goodbye to my pudgy puppy, we climbed into his black Crown Vic and headed toward The Gramercy, an upscale urban apartment complex on Garfield Place, where Veronica Henry had lived.

"I got an emailed copy of the Medical Examiner's report," Harry said, as we parked in front of the apartments. "Time of death was approximately three a.m. Our vic died of exsanguination due to sharp force trauma to the heart. A deep, angulated puncture wound to the back, between the fourth and fifth ribs, dissecting both the right and left ventricles."

"A quick death. Somebody knew what they were doing."

"My thoughts exactly," Harry said, as we rode the elevator to the sixth floor.

Veronica Henry's apartment, number 618, was easy to spot. Yellow crime scene tape still draped the door. I suspected the building's highbrow residents weren't too happy about that. But once Harry and I finished up today, the tape would disappear, along with any other trace of the victim, and their lives would return to normal.

We turned Veronica's apartment inside out and upside down, looking for anything the forensic folks might have missed. They'd come up empty on trace evidence. Harry would be checking into her financial records, cell phone, and computer. We were looking for the not so obvious. Oddball clues that might have gone unnoticed. Veronica's vague reference to 'the book' certainly wasn't much to go on. And her emphasis on the word 'stretch' seemed downright random. These were obviously important pieces to the puzzle. But how those pieces fit together was anyone's guess.

The apartment didn't show signs of a struggle. No furniture overturned, nothing knocked off her table tops. The pillows on her couch were still perfectly fluffed. Everything seemed in order, other than the gruesome pool of blood on the bedroom carpet where Veronica had bled out. She was taken quickly, quietly and efficiently.

We left the apartment an hour after we arrived with nothing to show for our efforts. I remembered Harry's bet that he would find something the others had missed. He looked so dejected when we left that I didn't have the heart to rub it in.

We split up and spent the next hour canvassing Veronica's neighbors, hoping someone might have heard or seen something unusual. Harry handed me a stack of his cards and headed for the top three floors. I took the bottom three. If no one answered, I left a note on the back of one of Harry's cards and shoved it beneath the door. Bottom line, we came up snake eyes.

This gumshoe-detective schtick was grinding on my last nerve. It was slow and tedious. Nothing like on TV. We were spinning our wheels while the clock ticked away, no closer to solving the case than before we'd started.

While we stood on the sidewalk licking our wounds, Harry pulled out his case notes and plotted our next move. "I'm still waiting on Veronica's phone records. Let's go chat with her next of kin. Maybe see if we can dig up some friends."

I noticed movement in a window, just over his right shoulder, in the adjacent building. I leaned to my left, putting Harry between me and whoever found us so interesting. "Don't turn around. We're being watched."

"We are?"

"Next building down. Third floor, fifth window across."

I shifted slightly, peered across his shoulder, and stifled a laugh. Our snoop had gray hair and tiny facial features. She also wore wire-rim glasses, which I only saw because she lowered a set of binoculars from her face. Every neighborhood had one. Some ancient fossil who had nothing better to do than spy on the comings and goings of their neighbors — aka Mrs. Nussbaum.

"A boilermaker says I just found our witness."

Harry grinned. "My kind of bet. You're on."

"Put your arm through mine. We're taking a leisurely stroll next door."

Canvassing neighbors at a crime scene is a hit-or-miss undertaking. Maybe our gum-grinding busybody was out that night. Not likely though with the time of death in the vicinity of three a.m. Or maybe the badges talked to her and she denied seeing anything. But if that was the case, I'd call bullshit.

Rubbernecking grannies like her never sleep. They're up all night peeing.

We didn't want our spy to know we were coming, so we took the steps instead of the elevator. Harry counted doors, calculating which apartment we needed. "3B," he whispered and pointed down the hallway.

Harry rapped on the door a few times and got no response. He rapped a little harder, leaned in close and barked, "CPD."

A rustling noise drifted into the hall from the other side of the door. I tugged at Harry's sleeve as a shadow inside the apartment blocked the light beneath the door. Harry raised his hand to knock again.

"Oh, for fuck's sake." I pounded on the door. "C'mon, lady. Open up! We know you're in there."

A few seconds later, the metallic click-clack of a sliding deadbolt filled the hall. The door opened a few inches and a tiny voice croaked, "Yes?"

Harry jostled me aside. "Detective Harry Delk with CPD, ma'am. We're investigating a homicide. May we come in and ask you a few questions?"

"I'm afraid I don't know anything about that poor girl's death next door. Sorry."

The oldster tried to shut the door, but I'd wangled my foot across the threshold. "Listen, Snoopy McSnoopster. Ain't nothing happens on this street you don't know about. You know how I know that? I've got a blue-hair just like you living next door to me. I can't take a — Hey!"

Harry had hip-checked me away from the door. "What my partner meant to say, ma'am, is that we noticed you at your window, taking an...intense interest in the activity on your street. Why, I'll bet you're a part of the neighborhood watch, aren't you? Thank heaven for you folks. We couldn't do our jobs without you."

The door opened wide. In front of us stood a four-foot-five

tribble wearing a housecoat and slippers. The smile on her face made it clear that Harry had struck the right chord with his ass-kissing happy crap. Smoke wafted through the room from a still-burning cigarette, resting in an ashtray, on a table beside the window. Next to the ashtray sat her binoculars.

"Why, thank you, Officer. Please come in. I'm Ada Pike, and I do belong to the neighborhood watch. In fact, I'm the coordinator for this entire street."

I snorted, but Harry pressed on. "Did you happen to catch any suspicious activity three nights ago — the night of the murder?"

The tribble glared at me from the corner of her eye then shifted her gaze to Harry. I swear little pink hearts exploded from her head.

"Well, as a matter of fact, I did, now that you mention it. It must have been two a.m. No, wait," she said. "Let me check." She pulled a tattered notebook from the pocket of her house-coat. "It was five after three. See it says so, right here in my notes. I recorded it because I didn't recognize the man or the car."

I thought Harry was going to kiss her. "Think hard, ma'am. What did he look like? Would you know him again if you saw him?"

"Maybe. It was awfully dark. He had one of those big fancy-schmancy sedans. White, I think." She pointed out the window. "Parked it on the opposite side of the street, not far from that telephone pole. I should have jotted down the plate number. Not like me to miss a thing like that."

"Did you see anything else that might help us, Mrs. Pike? Or hear anything unusual?"

"No. I'm sorry. But I'll keep my eyes open. I'm so happy I could help you, Detective Delk."

Every time she looked at Harry her crinkly eyes sparkled like diamonds. All I'd gotten were beady-eyed glares.

Harry handed her one of his cards as she walked us to the door. "Give me a call if you remember anything else, ma'am. And thank you for your service on the neighborhood watch."

Suck up.

"I'll do just that, Detective. Drop by any time. Bye-bye, now." She snarled and flipped me the bird as she closed the door. I knew where I stood.

Our next stop would be at Veronica's parents' house. I checked my cell phone messages when we climbed back into Harry's car, and found that Dallas had called to give me the night off. Tuesdays were his slow nights, he'd said. He could handle the crowd. I wasn't sure how to feel about that. I needed the money, but I'd been burning the candle at both ends. Maybe a night of rest wouldn't be such a bad thing.

We climbed the steps to the modest brick house at 1326 Glenway Avenue and rang the bell. A woman in her mid-fifties came to the door. One look at her doe eyes and delicate features told me she had to be Veronica's mother. Harry introduced us, then extended our condolences and asked if she had a moment to chat. When she let us in, we found ourselves in the middle of a gathering of relatives. They were planning Veronica's service for the following day. Harry offered to come back another time, but I knew in my heart, he hoped they'd be willing to share any information they might have sooner rather than later.

It didn't feel right, being there among them, and yet what better chance could we have at speaking to the people closest to her? The family agreed to help us in any way they could. Hoping to cause as little disruption as possible, Harry and I moved to the kitchen to conduct our interviews.

One by one, we asked each of them in to chat, a brother, two sisters, and a cousin, leaving mom and dad for last. Harry handled the interviews skillfully and respectfully, choosing his words with compassion. Just because the family knew what

Veronica did for a living didn't mean they wanted her dragged through the mud.

Her siblings and cousin agreed that, over the years, Veronica had pulled away, keeping some distance between them. They all said it wasn't for lack of love. More like she didn't want to let them close enough to see the seedier side of her life. They were cooperative to a one, but in the end, told us nothing of value. They couldn't give us a list of her friends and came up blank when asked about any book that might have held particular meaning for her. Even Tom, Veronica's father, spoke of the same growing distance, which didn't surprise me. I doubted that Veronica would want her daddy to know sordid details about her line of work.

Alice Henry spoke lovingly about Veronica. "I was eighteen when I had my baby girl. Such a joy, she was." Alice's bittersweet memories ended with the same tale of separation. Just when I thought we'd struck out, her eyes lit up. "I'd nearly forgotten. It seemed so inconsequential at the time." She rose from her chair. "Excuse me, please. I'll be right back."

I stared silently at Harry, perched on the edge of his chair, steely-eyed and resolute, waiting for what might be our first solid clue.

Moments later, Alice returned, clutching an envelope. "Ronnie — that's what we called our daughter — told me to hang onto this. She said not to open it, to just put it away and forget it. And I almost did." Tears slid down her face as she gazed at the manila envelope in her hand. "She said if something ever happened to her, she wanted me to have this."

Instead of reaching for the envelope, Harry reached for her hand. "Thank you, Alice, for talking to us today and for remembering. I have to take this with me now. It's evidence. But once the investigation is finished, it will be returned to you. That's a promise."

She wiped her cheek, then placed the envelope in his hand.

"Mrs. Henry," I said quietly. "Did Veronica happen to mention recently that she'd come into any information? The kind that might...make her nervous?"

Alice's eyes shifted to the floor. "No. But like I said, we hadn't spoken in a while. And even when we did speak, she held a lot back. I think she didn't want to worry us."

I thanked Alice for her time and watched as she wandered back into the living room to rejoin her family. The odds of her knowing the details of Veronica's mystery dirt had been slim to none. But the question had needed to be asked.

I sat at the Henry's old Formica table with a lump in my throat, reminding myself that there are no tears in zombie hunting. I had spent years compartmentalizing — conditioning myself so I could do the job and still sleep at night.

Damn you, Harry Delk. Nobody makes me cry. Nobody.

10

SO, YOU'RE THE ASSHOLE?

Miriam spied Harry and me rounding the corner. She bolted from her chair and scrambled to block Cap's door.

"Captain Dorsey is reviewing the budget this afternoon. I'm afraid whatever you wish to discuss will have to wait. May I suggest you schedule an appointment now? *Before you leave.*" She darted her eyes back down the hallway, in case we'd missed her invitation to disappear.

"Where's the fun in that?" I asked, barreling around her desk.

A quick fake to her right pulled her from her post. One spin-move later, I was rapping on Cap's door. That fussy little office troll was too easy to screw with. She gasped as I chucked her rulebook to the curb and barged into Cap's office without his blessing.

"I tried, sir," Miriam whined. "I truly did. She's just..."

"Yes, Miriam," he said with a sigh. "She truly is."

Cap glanced up at me perched on the corner of his desk, then shifted his gaze toward Harry still hovering in the doorway.

"Nighthawk. How can I help you today?" Cap rubbed his chin and held up a folder labeled *Fiscal Budget*. "A raise perhaps? An advance? A requisition for munitions? Napalm?"

"Not yet, sir. But soon."

Harry closed the door and announced the reason for our visit. "We've got our first leads in the Henry murder investigation."

Cap tossed the budget report aside and laid his glasses on his desk. "Do tell?"

Taking one of the cracked, red vinyl chairs across from Cap's desk, Harry explained, "One of the vic's neighbors, a crime-stopper type, spotted a white luxury car parked nearby around three a.m. But she didn't get the plate number. Could be something. Maybe not. And we interviewed the Henry family. Veronica gave her mother an envelope containing the name of an offshore bank, an account number, and a passcode."

"That's a start. Make sure you book the contents into evidence. Wouldn't want that to go missing."

"Already done, Cap."

"Well, get on it then. Don't stand here talking to me. I'm busy," he said, rolling his eyes. "With stupid shit."

Miriam shot daggers at me as we left Cap's office. I smiled sweetly and told her to have a good day.

"Why do you torment her?" Harry asked, when we'd made it out of earshot.

"It's a sickness."

We were halfway to Harry's desk before I noticed Craig Farragut marching toward us. The freaking douche-canoe. What was he doing at the 51st?

Harry nudged me. "Here comes the reason you didn't get your order to raise."

"You mean the reason I got arrested."

"Craig, how's it going?" Harry asked, shaking hands with the bastard.

"You tell me. Any leads in the Henry case?"

I elbowed in-between them. "Aren't you going to introduce me to your friend, Harry?"

"Allie Nighthawk," Harry said, shooting me a warning glance, "DA, Craig Farragut."

Farragut's eyes flashed. "Ah, yes. The...cadaver diver."

"Always nice to meet a fan."

"Raise any more corpses since your arraignment?"

"No. It's been slow," I said with a shrug. "So, you're the ass—"

"Actually," Harry interrupted. "We're making headway on the case. We just got our first solid lead on an offshore account that belonged to the vic. It's only a matter of time."

Farragut's eyes never left mine. "Really? Glad to hear it. Did that book ever turn up, Ms. Nighthawk? The one Ms. Henry mentioned during your...inadmissible conversation?"

"No, it didn't. It was probably a red herring anyway."

Farragut's smile faded. "You'll have to excuse me. I'm late for a meeting. Nice to finally meet you, Ms. Nighthawk. Good luck at your hearing."

I watched that dickweed saunter down the hallway, in his freshly pressed Armani, and I marveled at how even his walk looked arrogant. Little Allie swore I was pissing vinegar because he'd had me arrested. But as usual, she was full of shit. The man was too smooth, too slick — too Brooks Brothers. There was more than met the eye behind that perfect, bleached smile and those piercing green eyes. Sooner or later, he and I would come to blows. It was just a matter of when. But in the meantime, Harry and I had a murderer to catch.

We sat at Harry's desk and hovered over his computer, pulling up Veronica's offshore account. Harry whistled when he read the balance.

"Man, I'm in the wrong business."

I peered over his shoulder at the monitor and almost

choked. Twenty-three-year-old Veronica Henry was worth in excess of a million-five. Harry checked her personal accounts, too. They had balances exceeding 50K.

I knew high-priced call girls made good money. Even great money. But socking away this kind of dough? She wasn't just boinking johns. What the hell had she been up to? And was that what had gotten her murdered?

Harry swiveled his chair toward me. "You really think the book's a red herring?"

"Yes. No. Maybe. I don't know. Maybe it's not a book, per se. Maybe it's a ledger. With all that scratch laying around, you'd think she'd keep a record of it somewhere."

Harry pulled up his email and smiled. "The phone records are here. Shall we?"

The list could be sorted by date, time and number. We were able to view both Veronica's outgoing and incoming calls on the day of her death. When we sorted the list by source, I was surprised at how many calls involved the same numbers.

"Escorts like her have a repeat clientele," Harry explained.

I stifled a yawn and looked at my watch. It was almost five o'clock. "This is going to take a while. Any chance we can check these out tomorrow?"

"Feeling like a boilermaker?"

"Maybe two."

As we got up to leave, my phone rang. It was Opie. When I heard what he had to say, my mouth went dry.

"That's up to you," I said. "If you're ready, I'm ready. Let's get this over with. See you then."

I shoved my phone back into my pocket and sighed. "Make that three boilermakers. The Prosecutor's Office had a scheduling conflict with the preliminary hearing on January 16th. They asked Opie if we could go forward tomorrow morning. Nine a.m. sharp. Opie says he's ready."

"Boilermakers it is." Harry grabbed his jacket from the back of his chair, and we headed out the door.

11

———

THE TIP OF THE ICEBERG

Dallas looked surprised to see Harry and me saunter into The Blue Note for our afternoon cocktails. Jimmy and Hank sat at the bar, sipping beer and playing Keno. The booths and tables were empty. Apparently, Dallas hadn't been lying. Tuesdays were slow. But I wasn't there to work. A cool, smooth Jack Daniel's on the rocks (or two) would ease me into my night off.

Within an hour, the early crowd left and made way for the late afternoon drinkers. Business picked up a bit. I almost offered to help, but Dallas handled it like a pro. Harry stepped out to pick up his shirts at the dry cleaners before they closed at seven but promised he'd return.

I kibitzed with Dallas between customers, sipping my Jack and wondering what fresh hell awaited me in the courtroom come morning. As I was picturing myself being led away in cuffs, a suit slid onto the barstool next to mine. Spiffy dresser, haughty, straight out of GQ. The kind of guy who never sits next to me intentionally. (Coincidentally, the kind of guy who sets my teeth on edge). I looked over my shoulder, thinking he was trying to hit on some high-class hunny on the other side of me. When that wasn't the case, I stared down at my drink, hoping Mr. GQ would take the hint. Fat chance.

"Ms. Nighthawk?" The suit scooted his stool closer to mine. "May I buy you a drink?"

"No."

He sat back stunned, but recovered in a beat and shot me a thin-lipped smile. "I assure you, this isn't a pickup. I have a business proposition for you."

That's when I noticed Harry had returned and had taken a stool a couple of seats over, pretending to be a fly on the wall. He turned his back to me but was obviously listening to my conversation.

I swiveled my stool toward GQ and scanned him, head to toe. He was stylish and neat as a pin, all right. But his eyes were cold and hawk-like, his barely there smile fresh from the freezer. Little Allie got her panties in a wad. *Who is this guy? What kind of proposition?* There was only one way to find out.

"I'm listening," I said.

"I understand you're working the Veronica Henry murder."

How had he known that? Intrigued, I sipped my Jack and played along. "And if I am?"

"I represent a local businessman who is concerned that certain *information* may come to light that could *tarnish* his reputation."

"That's the way investigations go sometimes. Especially murder investigations."

"My client is a wealthy man. He's willing to pay a lot of money for that information. Even more for that same information on other...involved parties."

"What makes you so sure there's information to be had?"

GQ chuckled. "Ms. Henry was many things. Sexy, discreet. But above all, smart. She understood that information equals power. My client paid for her services, as well as her silence. Now that she's dead, her continued silence is assured. But the information she possessed is still out there, somewhere. My client wants it. Now. All of it."

"And if I don't want to play?"

"That would be a grave mistake."

I side-eyed him. "How do I know that you, or your client, didn't kill Veronica?"

"We had no reason to want her dead. The quid pro quo arrangement suited everyone just fine. Her death, on the other hand, is problematic."

GQ pulled a card from his pocket and laid it on the bar. "My employer's offering more than you could ever hope to make puppeteering corpses. Call me when you've found the *merchandise*."

He slunk away as stealthily as he had appeared, leaving only his business card behind. I picked it up and turned it over. The card was blank, except for a handwritten phone number.

Harry, and his bottle of Guinness, were at my elbow in an instant. "So, Andre Petrov wants to buy any confidential information we turn up. That's interesting."

"Who's Petrov?"

"He's a lieutenant with the Russian mob."

I tucked Petrov's business card in my pocket and whistled. "Veronica sure had some interesting clients."

"Not to mention a lot of them," Harry said. He chugged the rest of his Guinness and plunked the bottle onto the bar. "Odds are, this is just the tip of the iceberg."

Wasn't that peachy? If we were right, we might end up with more suspects than we could shake a stick at.

12

———

NANI NANI BOO BOO

Come 9 a.m., Opie and I resumed our seats on the bench outside Hearing Room A and waited for our case to be called.

Opie hummed quietly, staring into space, tapping his foot against the marble floor, over and over again. Counselor Sling Blade looked like he'd slipped over the edge. The wheel was spinning but the hamster was dead.

I covered my face with my hands and stifled a moan. Then I drove my palm into the top of his knee, bringing the tapping to an end. "Relax. You look like a two-year-old who has to pee."

"We're back in front of Judge Franklin, you know."

And things had gone so swimmingly last time. "Suck it up," I hissed. "You've got nowhere to go but up."

The announcement of my case blared over the PA system, causing me to twitch like a freaking freshie. Opie and I entered the courtroom and took our places at the defense table.

Opie straightened his tie and nodded curtly to Jerry Milligan across the aisle.

The Clerk of Courts rose to his feet. "All rise. The Criminal Court of Hamilton County is now in session. The Honorable

Harold T. Franklin presiding. Please be seated and come to order."

Judge Franklin flipped open his file and leaned toward his microphone. "Good morning. In the matter of the State of Ohio versus Allie Nighthawk, is the defendant prepared to formally enter a plea at this time?"

Opie nodded. "Yes, Your Honor."

Judge Franklin stared at me over the top of his tortoise-shelled cheaters. "Ms. Nighthawk, it is charged that on or about January 5th , in the city of Cincinnati, Ohio, you did knowingly and willfully raise the corpse of one deceased Veronica Henry without an order of authorization, in violation of O.R.C. 2927.01, subsection B, gross abuse of a corpse: 'No person, except as authorized by law, shall treat a human corpse in a way that would outrage reasonable community sensibilities.' How do you plead?"

Opie kicked my foot beneath the table, reminding me to answer like a sane person this time.

"Not guilty, Your Honor." I glanced over my shoulder and found Harry seated in the back row. He smiled and tossed me a wink.

Judge Franklin nodded toward Milligan. "Mr. Prosecutor, call your first witness."

"The State would like to call Doctor William Francis Blanchard to the stand."

My heart sank as Doc Blanchard strutted up the center aisle. After the clerk swore him in, he sat in the witness chair with his chin held high, radiating confidence and grim determination. I remembered our conversation from the day of the raising when he said he would deny having given me authorization to raise Veronica Henry. All I could do was stare straight ahead, hold my breath, and hope he wouldn't torpedo me.

Milligan cleared his throat and launched his attack. "Doctor Blanchard, please state your name for the record."

"Dr. William Francis Blanchard, the third."

"Thank you, Doctor. Now if you would, please review your curriculum vitae for the court."

When Doc finished rambling off the alphabet soup of his degrees and certifications, Milligan continued. "Doctor Blanchard, were you present in your morgue on January 5th, awaiting a court order to authorize the raising of the corpse of Ms. Veronica Henry?"

"Yes, sir."

"Was Ms. Nighthawk with you?"

"Yes, sir."

"Did you, in fact, receive the court order which authorized the raising of said corpse?"

Doc glanced at me. "No, sir."

"And despite the lack of said order, did Ms. Nighthawk, in fact, proceed to raise the corpse of Ms. Henry?"

"Yes, sir."

"In the absence of said warrant, did you, in your capacity as Medical Examiner, give Ms. Nighthawk express permission to raise the corpse of Ms. Henry?"

Doc hesitated, staring down at his hands folded in his lap. "No, sir."

Milligan stepped toward the stand. "I'm sorry, Doctor Blanchard, would you please repeat your answer? Louder this time, for the court, if you please."

"No, sir. I did not."

"Thank you, Doctor Blanchard. I have no further questions at this time."

Judge Franklin glanced at Opie. "Would the defense like to cross-examine the witness?"

"Yes, Your Honor." Opie stood and approached the stand. "Doctor Blanchard, would you agree that you have testified here today that you were present with Ms. Nighthawk when she raised the corpse of Veronica Henry?"

"Yes, sir."

"Did you, in fact, tell Ms. Nighthawk that in your capacity as Medical Examiner, you did not think an order to raise was required?"

Doc fidgeted with a button on his sport coat. 'Yes, sir. I did."

"Did you further advise Ms. Nighthawk that it was in your purview as Medical Examiner to authorize the raising of the corpse of Veronica Henry to assist you in determining the cause of her death?"

"Yes, sir."

"When Ms. Nighthawk took you at your word and rose Veronica Henry, did you at any time try to stop her?"

Doc squirmed. "No, sir."

Milligan tossed his pen onto his notepad. "Objection! Dr. Blanchard sharing his *opinion* with Ms. Nighthawk that he is entitled to authorize a raising without the requisite order is not the same as him providing her with express consent to raise!"

"Your Honor, please!" Opie glared at Milligan. "I'm trying to—"

"Overruled, for the moment," the judge said. "I want to see where the defense is going. Proceed, Counselor."

Opie cleared his throat and picked up where he left off. "Did you, in fact, Dr. Blanchard, encourage Ms. Nighthawk to 'get the raising over with' because you had a 'full house and no open tables'?"

Doc's cheeks blazed. "Damn straight, I did. All this bureaucratic nonsense has to stop. I've got enough on my hands without having to fight the damn County just to do my job. As long as I serve in the role of Medical Examiner, I'm legally and ethically bound to perform a complete examination of a corpse to determine cause of death. And that includes authorizing a raising if I deem it necessary."

"Final question, Doctor. Did you deem the raising of Ms. Henry necessary?"

Doc turned his head and stared into my eyes. "Yes, sir. I did."

Opie smiled. "Thank you, Dr. Blanchard. I have no further questions."

Judge Franklin nodded to Milligan. "Further questions for the witness, Mr. Prosecutor?"

"Yes, Your Honor." Jerry took his time strolling toward the witness stand. "Dr. Blanchard, once Ms. Nighthawk raised the corpse of Veronica Henry, did you glean any additional information that assisted you in the determination of the cause of her death?"

"Not as such."

"Thank you, Doctor Blanchard. No further questions."

The judge scribbled a note in his file. "The witness may step down."

Doc slid out of the witness stand, kept his eyes front and center, and returned to his seat.

Judge Franklin glanced out over the bench. "Will you be calling additional witnesses, Mr. Prosecutor?"

"No, sir," Milligan said, backing away from the stand and returning to his table.

"Mr. Andrews, will the Defense be calling any witnesses today?"

Opie shook his head. "No, Your Honor."

"Very well. Closing remarks. Mr. Prosecutor?"

"Your Honor," Milligan began, "This whole dog and pony show has been nothing but a smoke screen. Clearly, a request was made for an order to raise. That request was denied. Ms. Nighthawk proceeded with the raising without the required legal authorization to do so. Those are the facts of this case, and they are not in dispute. The prosecution rests."

Judge Franklin nodded to Opie. "Mr. Andrews?"

Opie climbed to his feet. "Your Honor, it is our contention that while the DA's office was approached for an order to raise, no such order was required. It is further our contention that the Medical Examiner is legally and ethically bound to perform a complete examination of a corpse to determine cause of death, and that by the authority of his office, he may order the raising of a corpse if he deems the resultant evidence could assist him in his determination of cause of death."

Milligan flung his legal pad across the table. "You've got to be kidding." He rubbed his face with his hands, then leaned back into the mic. "Your client's request to secure an order to raise was denied because you had no basis to assume the corpse could attest to her own cause of death. And even if the corpse could provide such evidence, the testimony of the undead isn't admissible in court."

"I've heard enough," said the judge. "I concur with Doctor Blanchard's assessment on both counts. I believe he properly construed the authority he carries as the acting Medical Examiner of Hamilton County. And I agree that the bureaucratic red tape civil servants have to wade through, simply to function in the commission of their duties, is egregious and must end. And this is where it starts. Charges dismissed." The judge banged his gavel.

I think I peed a little.

Milligan's jaw dropped. "But Your Honor. There was no order to raise."

"Save it, Counselor. In case you missed it, I made my ruling. Charges are dismissed."

Opie grinned and quickly swept his notes into his briefcase, as if he were afraid the judge would call a do-over.

"Nice job, Counselor," I said, skirting past him. "Worth every nickel I paid. I'll be right back."

Harry lingered at the doorway chatting with Doc Blanchard. I wanted to speak to them both. I reached them just in time to hear Harry say, "I read your report. What kind of murder weapon would inflict that kind of wound?"

"A long wide blade," Doc said, shoving his briefcase beneath his arm. "Maybe a hunting knife, or some kind of military blade."

He stepped past Harry on his way out the door.

"Dr. Blanchard," I called, tapping him on the shoulder. "Thank you for today."

He barely turned his head. "Don't thank me, Ms. Nighthawk. I told you I wouldn't lie for you, and I didn't. You should be thankful that your attorney asked the right questions."

He slipped out the door without another word, leaving my gratitude hanging in the wind.

I waved to the back of his head as he walked away. "You're welcome, Allie."

Harry clapped me on the shoulder. "Don't mind Doc. He took a turn on the hot seat, but he didn't get burned. No harm, no foul."

I smiled and pointed toward the street. "What do you say we deliver the good news to Cap? In case he couldn't hear Farragut's screams when Milligan had to tell him that he'd lost the case."

Little Allie lectured me, insisting that I wipe the grin off my face. I told her to shut her pie hole.

Nani nani boo boo, you stinking brain bitch. I won.

13

HOW MANY ZOMBIES IN A HORDE?

The formidable Miriam Miller looked fetching, as always, in her black pencil skirt and crisp, white, button-down blouse. Her hair, pulled back from her face so tightly that her eyes went almond-shaped, was once again shellacked into a bun at the top of her head.

Harry and I had barely rounded the corner when her head popped up from her desk. She swung her long, skinny neck in our direction and stared at us with her beady little eyes, reminding me of a turkey vulture tracking its prey.

She vaulted from her chair, in an impressive burst of speed, and rapped on Cap's door. Before he could even respond, she called, "Harry Delk and that...that...Nighthawk woman are here to see you, sir. Are you in?"

Cap's voice drifted through the solid oak door. "What difference would that make, Miriam? She'll make her way in here. She always does."

I flashed the crimson-faced Miriam a victorious smirk as I swept past her into Cap's office. Harry followed a few steps behind, making sure to say, *excuse me,* when he squeezed past the ferocious admin-bouncer.

"Good news," I said, making myself at home in one of his ratty vinyl chairs. I plopped my feet on the corner of his desk and flaunted a shameless smile. "I won. Take that DA Farragut. You messed with the wrong corpse whisperer."

Cap folded his fingers beneath his chin and gazed at me with tired red eyes. "So, I've already heard, strangely enough, from DA Farragut. I understand the futility in these words even as they tumble from my mouth, but you need to keep a low profile for a while. Actually, you need to be invisible. You've shit in his oatmeal enough for one lifetime."

Me, low profile? Invisible? What were the odds?

When I didn't respond, Cap pushed the issue. "Have I made myself clear?"

"Crystal," I said, ignoring Little Allie, who threatened to slap me for telling a bald-faced lie.

Cap leaned back in his chair and fixed his eyes on Harry. "Where are we on the Henry case?"

"Andre Petrov stopped in at The Blue Note and had a chat with Nighthawk last night."

"The mob lieutenant? How does he fit into the puzzle?"

"Veronica's book, maybe," I said. "Petrov seemed to think our investigation would turn up some very valuable, very private information. He was willing to pay big bucks for it."

Cap snorted. "Have you considered that Petrov might be the murderer? Maybe the dirt she wanted to share was about him."

"He claims he had no reason to kill her. Veronica and his boss had a *mutually acceptable arrangement*."

"Do you believe him?"

"I don't know. The point is, whatever she had on Petrov's boss is up for grabs now. And if Veronica's book is filled with that kind of sensitive information, we could have an entire smorgasbord of suspects."

"So, find the damn book. Anything else?"

Harry cleared this throat. "I got the phone records yesterday. I need to analyze them. See what direction they take me."

"And yet, you're here because..."

"Right." Harry did an about face. "Call you later, partner."

Harry's footsteps clacked against the tile as he retreated to his office.

Fearing I could be shanghaied for yet another assignment, I held up my hands in protest. "Don't look at me, Cap. I did my thing. I haven't gotten a full night's sleep in a week."

"That reminds me," he said, sliding open his desk drawer. "I have something for you."

He handed me a business envelope — with a check in it. I felt a little woozy.

"This covers your services to date. Don't get used to getting paid so quickly." Cap glanced back down to whatever he'd been working on when we'd come in. "I pushed it through for an off-cycle check, only because you whined about being broke. That won't happen again."

I left Cap's office a new woman. I even planted a big wet one on Miriam's over-powdered cheek as I danced by her desk. She recoiled faster than a mongoose.

Dollar signs pinged through my brain like pinballs. That always happens when money finds its way into my pocket. Fiscal responsibility is for diehard conservatives, not kickass corpse whisperers. Clothes? Forget about it. Black jeans, well-worn T-shirts and a ball cap. That's how I roll. Spa day? Hell, no. Who can handle a gun with long acrylic nails?

That left only one option: the firing range.

***

I walked into Brasshole's and smiled as a wave of burnt gun powder filled my nose. Beats the crap out of Chanel No. 5, any day.

I bought some targets and sent them twenty yards downrange on the T-rail, listening to the gunfire that flanked me on either side. I closed my eyes and relaxed. A peacefulness came over me.

This. This was where I belonged. In a place where guns did most of the talking, not mouths. And where what little *was* said stayed in the range, like the bullets trapped inside its cinderblock walls.

I pulled Hawk, aimed, and let him eat his way through the first three mags. Then I slid my backup piece, Baby, a Glock 26 from my ankle holster and had more fun. While everyone around me shot center mass, I obliterated the heads from my targets. That's called doing it zombie style. It didn't take me long to burn through the targets and my ammo. Much as I would have loved to spend the rest of my day, as well as my paycheck, playing with my toys, I decided to head home to let Headbutt know I was alive. And maybe catch a quick nap before heading to The Blue Note for my shift.

Nobody would ruin my perfect afternoon, not even Nonnie Nussbaum. I killed the Lowrider's engine about thirty yards from my driveway and walked the bike home, feeling the sun on my cheeks, and daring myself to feel hopeful for the first time since I'd returned to the Queen City. I twisted the knob on the kitchen door.

Nonnie sprang up from behind the fence like a seventy-year-old jack-in-the-box. "Mrs. Nighthawk! Look! Your naughty, naughty golem killing my rose bushes."

"Sorry, Mrs. Nussbaum. I'll have a talk with Headbutt... again."

I hurried inside before I caught another ration of shit and slammed the door behind me. But Headbutt, who hadn't been outside since early morning, pawed furiously at the weather stripping on the sill.

"This wouldn't be a problem if you behaved yourself," I said, yanking the door back open.

Headbutt's eyes twinkled.

"Don't do it. Don't you even think about it."

He barked and wagged his stubby tail.

"I mean it."

Headbutt trotted out past me, head held high, a dog on a mission. Nonnie planted her feet shoulder-width apart on the other side of the fence and waited, garden hose in hand, ready for the day's skirmish in the Battle of the Bushes.

I let out a sigh and pulled the door closed. The two of them deserved each other. *Let the best golem win*, I thought, as I plopped on the couch and began a silent countdown to Nonniegeddon.

The melee commenced on cue, beginning with Nonnie's bloodcurdling war cry, followed closely by a raucous combination of barks and growls. The amazingly short-lived fracas ended with a thump at my kitchen door. I was half afraid it might be Nonnie, wanting to turn the hose on me, but it was only Headbutt, shaking the excess water from his coat.

I let him in and waggled my finger in his face. "You bring this on yourself, you know."

He sauntered past me without so much as a glance and plopped on his favorite register vent to soak up the heat.

Nonnie might have won the battle, but the war was far from over.

By the time I walked into The Blue Note, Dallas had stocked the bar and iced the tubs. I mopped the floor and rolled silverware to stay busy, until around nine, when Harry and Opie stopped in to buy me a congratulatory shot that magically turned into three.

I brought up the war between Nonnie and Headbutt, hoping someone might offer solutions that didn't involve duct-taping Nonnie's mouth or moving. The most surprising suggestion came from Harry.

"Get a bird."

"How's that going to help?"

"Oh, it won't," Harry said, taking a sip of his Guinness. "Birds are easier to take care of, is all I'm saying. You don't have to walk them. And they don't piss on your neighbor's bushes." He pulled out his phone and scrolled through some pictures. "This is Kulu, my African Grey."

Well, slap my silly ass and call me Sally! Harry had a pet. Go figure.

Harry rambled on about how smart his bird was. How it did tricks and talked a blue streak. His phone vibrated on the bar top, interrupting his story about how he taught the bird to sing "Drunk on a Plane."

Thank you, Lord. A freaking pterodactyl wasn't worthy of that much conversation, much less a stinking parrot.

Harry ended the call, drained the last of his beer and said, "We're up."

"You and me?" I said, looking at the clock. "Now?"

"Biter sighting at The Crosley Building."

I could feel Dallas's eyes burning a hole in the back of my head. I turned to apologize, but he waved me off. "You were doing more drinking than working anyway. I got this."

Well. That was just uncalled for. Even if it was true.

I swung by Dallas's office to grab Hawk and my Ka-Bar. A light snow had fallen, so it made more sense for me to ride with Harry than to take the Harley. The moment I climbed into the passenger seat of his car Little Allie started yapping my ear off. She had a hinky feeling about this call. So did I.

I buckled my seatbelt and asked, "Who calls in a biter sighting in an abandoned building at ten o'clock at night?"

"I asked the same question," Harry said. "Anonymous caller from a pay phone, a block north."

"A *pay phone?*"

Harry snorted. "They still exist, you know. Not everyone can afford cell phones."

He parked beneath a street light, maybe fifty feet from the corner of Spring Grove and Arlington, and radioed in our location. "1 David 26 out for investigation at 1329 Arlington Street."

I opened the car door and got a noseful of *Eau de Deadhead.*

"We're in the right place," I said, letting my eyes wash over the ten-story tall Crosley Building, a behemoth of crumbling brick and broken windows.

Harry slipped his radio into his pocket, then opened the glove compartment and pulled out his backup piece. He clipped it to his belt and took the lead as we jogged through the dark.

"Seriously?" I snickered, drawing Hawk. "Your back up piece is a .38, too?"

He puffed like a freight train. "Big surprise. I told you, I'm a dinosaur."

Something rustled to my right. I spun, holding Hawk at high ready. A piece of newspaper tumbled through the air and plastered itself against an ancient metal dumpster stationed along the Arlington Street side of the building.

I exhaled slowly and lowered my gun.

Little Allie harrumphed and called me a wussy.

"Bite me, bitch."

Harry glanced over his shoulder. "You say something?"

"No. Keep moving."

Stupid head hag.

From our left came the unmistakable sound of a footstep, as it crunched against the broken glass, bricks and concrete that littered the ground. Harry and I whirled, weapons drawn, but the art deco-styled building threw random shadows in the waning glow of the moon. Even with the help of a flashlight, scanning those inky silhouettes proved difficult — like distinguishing one shade of black against another.

One of the shadows rippled. Or had it? I shut my eyes and let my other senses go to work. The stink of death grew stronger. The air beside me displaced, and brushed silk-like against my skin. I shivered and tightened my grip on Hawk. "Harry?"

No answer.

"Harry."

"I can't see for shit," he muttered.

A biter popped into Harry's flashlight beam, maybe six feet ahead. In one fluid motion, he brought his .38 to bear, squeezed off a round, and nailed it between its eyes.

He drew in a long, loud breath and announced, "Deadhead down."

"Don't get cocky. Take a whiff," I said, breathing in the stench. "He's not the only game in town."

The sound of movement ahead in an archway spurred us forward. We reached the alcove and nearly tripped over splintered pieces of plywood strewn on the ground, directly across from an entrance to the building. Where once had been a boarded-up door, now stood a gaping black maw. A woman's scream came from inside.

Harry barked at his radio. "1 David 26, requesting backup. 1329 Arlington Street. Possible assault."

"Roger, 1 David 26. Backup en route."

"We don't have time to wait for backup," I whispered. "One bite and she's finished."

Harry snorted. "Who said anything about waiting? Get the hell behind me and see how dinosaurs do things."

Our flashlight beams created thin pinholes of light in the

black abyss. We stared into the void and funneled inside, eyes and ears peeled, creeping forward at the speed of slugs. Harry shined his light to the right, and I shined mine to the left, but our field of vision was nearly nonexistent. The echo of our footsteps told us the room was huge. A second scream rang out, followed by distant banging and clanging noises.

After clearing our point of entry, Harry and I headed in the direction of the scream and ended up at a large, heavy-gauge metal door. He yanked on the handle and pulled. The door groaned, but opened wide. Unseen feet shuffled across the concrete floor into the darkness. A distant chorus of moans and groans halted as we stepped through the doorway.

Little Allie, who hadn't been fond of this call to begin with, launched a full-scale assault in my head. She hadn't needed to. I was way ahead of her.

"Harry—"

"Yeah. I know. This is all kinds of FUBAR."

The huge metal door behind us slammed shut. That door weighed hundreds of pounds. It hadn't closed itself.

Harry brought the radio to his mouth. "1 David 26, 1329 Arlington Street. Where the hell is that backup? Possible zombie horde. Repeat. Possible zombie horde."

"Roger, 1 David 26," the dispatcher responded. "How...how many zombies in a horde?"

Harry looked at me and rolled his eyes.

"How the hell should we know?" I yelled into Harry's phone, *"Just send backup, damn it. Like everybody you got."*

Harry harrumphed and slid the radio back into his pocket. "Are you fucking kidding me? Did she really ask how many biters in a—"

He raised his .38 and fired. A bullet screamed past my head. I grabbed my aching ears and spun to find a biter flat on its back, not three feet behind me. Most of its head was missing.

"Thanks," I said, massaging my ears. "This room is a freaking echo chamber."

Air whooshed from Harry's lungs as he crashed to the concrete floor on his back. A biter had tackled him by his knees. Harry's gun bounced out of his hand and skittered across the floor into the darkness. He kicked at the biter's face, driving the heel of his shoe into its nose. The deadhead flew backward and rolled off Harry. I placed Hawk's muzzle against the back of its head and pulled the trigger. Liquified zombie chum (what I call *zushi*) instantly plastered Harry's face.

"Thanks, partner," he said, wiping his cheeks. "Not that I'm complaining, but maybe next time, blast the brains away from me?"

He pulled his backup piece from his belt, as I helped him to his feet.

"Picky, picky, picky." I eyeballed his gun. "Tell me you carry speed loaders for that fossil."

"Two. But I've always found if you need more than one, you're a crappy shot. Well, either that or you're in deep shit."

"Shh. What's that noise?"

We stood back to back and shined our flashlights in random patterns, illuminating as much of the room as our beams allowed. A sound thrummed in the darkness. The sound grew louder, and louder still. Its source finally crept into view.

"Harry," I said, aiming Hawk at the front line of an approaching horde. "I think we're in deep shit."

"Holy Hannah," he whispered, moving beside me. "How many do you think there are?"

"Really? How the... Too damn many, Harry. *Way* too damn many."

His primary gun, centered in the beam of my flashlight, was less than twenty feet from the throng of rotters that shambled toward us.

"Cover me." I fired into the horde and sprinted toward his gun.

Harry fired at the sea of deadheads, picking them off like ducks in a shooting gallery. But just that quick, he stopped.

"What the hell?" I screamed, bending down to grab the gun. "Keep firing!"

"Sorry. Six-shooter."

The cylinder clicked as he dropped in a speed loader. By that time, I was close enough to Harry to hand him his gun. But the biters were hot on my heels. Harry continued firing with his left hand, grabbed the gun from me with his right, and started double-pumping lead.

I raised Hawk, emptied my mag and slammed in a new one. For every rotter we dropped, another took its place. We were quickly losing ground. Harry and I shuffled backwards. He stopped firing to drop in his last speed loader.

Beneath the din of the gunfire, came the deep metallic groan of the door that had closed behind us. Footsteps pounded the concrete floor, coming faster and closer. Flashlight beams bobbed up and down as several of Cincinnati's finest, guns ablaze, joined Harry and me.

"Headshots!" I screamed. "Headshots!"

Multiple rounds of ammo later, the last of the biters fell. Harry and I scrambled to find our female vic, calling for her repeatedly. But we never got an answer. Moments later, I nearly tripped over a CD player sitting in the middle of an otherwise empty floor.

"Over here," I called, as I squatted down and pressed the play button.

The same high-pitched scream that had drawn us inside blared from its speaker.

"Well now," I said, grinning up at Harry. "Looks like someone wants to play."

14

WELL, DON'T YOU HAVE SOME BIG-ASS BALLS?

Waking up to a ringing phone at ten in the morning blows, especially when you didn't get to bed until six a.m. Even then, the only reason I was allowed to leave The Crosley Building was because Harry had volunteered to handle the reports. By then, the late night snow had melted, so he drove me back to the bar to pick up my Harley.

I considered letting the call go to voice mail. But then I pictured the old dinosaur hunched over his desk, slogging through the mountain of paperwork the night's events had prompted, and guilted myself into picking up the phone. Had I known it was Doc Blanchard on the line, I'd have left him hanging 'til The Rapture. He hemmed and hawed before telling me the reason for his call.

"You want me to do *what*?" I said, rubbing sleep from my eyes.

"Raise a corpse."

"Really? Well, don't you have some big-ass balls?" I pulled the phone away from my ear, ready to end the call.

"Wait. Don't hang up."

"Doc, you made it pretty clear that I don't report to you. When was that, now? Oh, yeah. Yesterday. In court. Bye-bye."

"This is different—"

"Why? Because you want some—"

"They found a body this morning at The Crosley Building."

"Yeah. A ton of them. The deadheads we took down last night."

"No. A recently deceased, non-infected, human body."

That woke me up faster than coffee with a Red Bull chaser. "Where? How?"

"At the bottom of an open elevator shaft. There's a neck laceration but no sign of a struggle. No DNA and no trace on the body. I can't tell whether he accidentally stumbled into the shaft in the dark, and cut his neck on the machinery, or if someone slit his throat."

Suddenly I wanted to raise that corpse as much as Doc did — but not without a *get out of jail free* card in my hand. "You were ready to throw me to the wolves yesterday, Doc. You want that corpse raised, it's going to take a court order."

"Fine. Go through the proper channels. But do it quick. Once I autopsy this guy, he won't have a brain."

When Doc hung up, I called Harry. He knew the whole story because he'd been at the station when the forensics team called in the body. In fact, he had already launched a sneak attack on Farragut in the hallway to ask for the order. Harry said he hadn't called me because he didn't want to wake me up. But knowing him, he probably thought he had a better chance of getting the order without me. And he would have been right.

"Farragut shot me down," Harry said. "No surprise there. I was just about to go see Cap and bring him up to speed."

"Be there in twenty," I said, turning on the shower.

After sandblasting away any remnants of The Crosley Building, I climbed into a clean pair of jeans and my *Aim for the Brain* T-shirt. Then I coaxed Headbutt outside and gave him the

Allie eye as he trotted toward Nonnie's bushes. I didn't have time to deal with him getting the hose again. Headbutt wore a pouty face when he strolled back inside, as if I'd sucked the joy from his life.

I kickstarted my Lowrider and lit out of the driveway like my hair was on fire. By the time poor Nonnie flew out her front door to jump my shit, I'd be long gone. I smiled at the visual, and Little Allie scolded me, telling me I'm not half as slick as I think I am.

That freeloading bitch squats in my brain like a croaking toad, just waiting for me to screw up. She should save her breath, or better yet, go find another brain to bicker with. It's taken me twenty-six years to hone my attitude problem. Why mess with perfection?

I arrived at Harry's desk with three minutes to spare. We trekked down the hall to Cap's office, discussing the case. When we turned the final corner, I discovered that Miriam had repositioned her desk directly across from Cap's door. Anyone entering or leaving his office had to pass on either side of her. Apparently, Miriam was determined not to go down without a fight.

The old biddy had game.

I flashed a toothy grin and perched on the corner of her desk. "Good morning, Miriam."

She narrowed her eyes and sat a little taller. "We've covered this before, Ms. Nighthawk. You're not on the Captain's schedule. Now, if you'd like—"

"Really? I'm certain we made an appointment." I reached across the desk for her day planner.

She dove to her right and snatched it, leaving the left side of Cap's doorway open. I barged into his office with Harry on my heels, followed by what I presumed was the sound of Miriam's fist pounding her desktop. When I reached behind me and gently pushed the door closed, a clear, concise, *damn it,* rang out from the other side.

Cap shook his head. "I've never heard that woman cuss before."

"I have that effect on people," I said, handing Cap an invoice. "Before I forget, here's my bill for the Veronica Henry investigation."

Cap flung it back at me. "The Henry investigation? What the heck for? You didn't do any raising or putting down."

"Hey, time is money. Harry's not the only one working this investigation. I may be cheap, but I'm not free." I flipped my bill into his inbox, daring him to argue with me.

Cap pointed to the crappy visitor chairs. "Take a load off, boys and girls. We need to chat about last night."

As Harry and I took our seats, I figured the conversation would jump right to the biter trap. As usual, I was wrong. Cap leaned forward and darted his eyes from Harry to me, then back to Harry.

"You mind telling me why you didn't wait for backup before going in?"

Harry put his elbows on the arms of his chair and leaned forward. "A woman screamed from inside the building. We'd already put one biter down outside on the perimeter. I feared for her safety."

"But it wasn't a real woman. It was a recording."

"How the hell could we know that? We hadn't made it inside yet."

"You almost died out there," Cap said. "Nighthawk, too."

"It was a judgment call. I'd do it again. So would Nighthawk."

I nodded. "Damn straight. Wait 'til you see my bill for putting down half the horde."

Cap rubbed his eyes and sighed. "Between you, Harry, and your backup, you can't possibly know how many Zs you *personally* took down."

"A crap ton, that's how many."

"What is that? Like eight? Ten? Send me the damned bill and I'll look at it."

"A crap ton is a shit load, rounded up. Way, way up."

"Can we get back to our discussion on protocol, please? Harry, you fired shots outside to take down the first biter. You should have called for backup then."

Harry blanched. "It was a biter call, for God's sake. Shots *will* be fired. It's a given. We don't—"

"Wait just a minute," I barked. "This is what Harry and I do. Biters don't shoot back. Calling in extra badges for every undead call would be a waste of personnel. Harry called for the cavalry when he realized we were in trouble. End of story."

Cap settled back in his chair and ran a hand across his bald head. "Don't take this lightly. Every action we take on biter calls is scrutinized and second-guessed by the public, the media, and the ACLU — from actual raisings, to civilian attacks, to loss of emergency responders. We have to be able to justify every move we make, on every call."

"Understood," Harry said, with a nod. "What about today's request from Doc Blanchard? He wants Nighthawk to raise the guy they found at the bottom of the elevator shaft in The Crosley Building."

Cap's gaze shifted to me. "Doc says the trace they collected at the scene was negligible. The vic's wounds could be consistent with a fall-related event. Doc has no way to determine whether the fall was accidental, or if somebody helped our vic into the shaft. Even though Doc is officially requesting the raising, we should go for the court order. Just to be safe."

"No dice," I said. "Harry went to Farragut. He wasn't about to give us a court order after yesterday's hearing."

"Do we even need one? Doc said he's willing to authorize your services. Based on the judge's ruling, that should be enough."

I shot out of my seat like a bottle rocket. "One day, Doc wants to throw me under the bus, and the next day, he wants my services. Words like 'should be enough' don't give me the warm fuzzies."

"We could go around Farragut," Harry suggested. "Pursue the order ourselves without the DA's blessing."

I yanked my phone out of my pocket and dialed Opie. The call went straight to voice mail, so I left him a message.

"Opie. Nighthawk. Believe it or not, Doc Blanchard wants me to do a raising at his office today. We tried to get a court order, but Farragut denied the request. Doc's willing to verbally authorize my assistance. I'm feeling twelve kinds of hinky here. Call me. ASAP."

"What about last night's attack?" Cap asked. "How many biters did they find?"

Harry glanced at his notes. "That would be twenty-six."

I paced the floor behind Harry, shaking my head. "That call was shady from the get go. Who phones in a biter sighting at an abandoned building at ten o'clock at night? And *twenty-six* biters? I've never seen twenty-six biters hording in one place *ever,* let alone in Cincinnati. We're not exactly the rotter capital of the world."

Harry chuckled. "No pun intended, but the woman's scream coming from a CD player, in the middle of an abandoned warehouse, kind of screams setup."

"That's my point," I said. "Rotters have one driving need. They need to eat. They're not social butterflies. They don't mingle in groups like hangry party guests, hoping to stumble into a platter of brain crudités. Someone corralled those biters inside The Crosley Building and tried to serve us up as dinner."

Cap sighed and rubbed his forehead. "But who? And how?"

"Still working on that," I said. "But as for the why, we're obviously digging in the right places on the Henry investigation. What else could it be?"

Harry nodded. "I requested the vic's account balances and phone records. That request is on file. I haven't finished reviewing them yet, but it's only a matter of time. I'm betting someone is very nervous about what those records will show."

"Could be," Cap said. "What about the book Veronica Henry mentioned when you raised her. Have you located it? And have we ever figured out the significance of the word 'stretch'?"

Harry slumped in his seat. Dark circles crested beneath his bloodshot eyes. His normally clean-shaven cheeks were flecked with gray stubble. "Not yet," he murmured. "But we will."

Cap's phone rang, interrupting our meeting. He took the call, responding with a series of grunts and monosyllabic words. After hanging up quickly, he pushed his chair back, got to his feet, and grabbed elevator guy's evidence bag from the desktop.

"Doc Blanchard would like to meet with us in the ME's office. He says he's got a proposition for you, Nighthawk."

15

NOBODY LIKES ANKLE-BITERS

So, Doc had a proposition for me, did he? A host of possibilities flitted through my mind as Harry and I followed Cap's county car to the ME's office. None of those scenarios boded well for me. Visions of being handcuffed and led off to jail topped the list, followed closely by a tableau of Jade Chen skewering me on the nightly news.

I don't play well with others, particularly the press. And for whatever reason, Jade Chen's liberal, corpse-loving heart had declared war on me. She was more of a nuisance than a concern, really. Still, the brain bitch, intimately familiar with my ability to shoot off my mouth, remained vigilant, urging me to 'bite my tongue' whenever the media maven was near.

The three of us appeared at Doc's doorway, curious but wary.

He invited us to sit, then quickly got down to business. "Thank you all for coming. I understand your reluctance to take on another raising, Nighthawk. I think you may have... misinterpreted my willingness to testify on your behalf yesterday—"

I opened my mouth to protest, but he held up a finger and forged ahead.

"That is to say, perhaps I didn't express myself clearly. While it's true that I would not lie for you, or anyone, in court, I did not mean to imply that you had asked me to do so. Thankfully, your attorney asked the right questions, thereby allowing me to assist in your defense. I'm quite pleased with the outcome." He stopped his speech and stared at me with hawk-like eyes and a too-wide grin, reminding me of The Grinch.

I waggled a finger at him. "That's not exactly what you said on the day of the raising, is it? I seem to recall you saying that I did *not* act under your authority, and that you did *not* instruct me to raise Ms. Henry's corpse. And that if asked under oath, that would be your testimony."

Blanchard's chrome dome glistened with sweat. "It was a stressful time, Ms. Nighthawk. In retrospect, I could have been more supportive."

It was my turn to sport a shit-eating grin. "That's an understatement. Especially since I'm the one who got arrested."

"Cut to the chase," Cap said. "What is this proposition of yours?"

Doc shoved a piece of paper across his desk. "I've prepared a document for us to sign, stipulating that I am directing you, in my capacity as the ME, to raise Alejandro Vega. Cap and Harry can witness our signatures. I'll ask my clerk to notarize it."

"Who the hell is Alejandro Vega?" I asked.

Doc sighed. "The guy from the bottom of the elevator shaft."

Little Allie thought this notarized statement smelled like the hind end of a hippo. I wasn't crazy about the idea either. But Doc swore it would protect me.

"You heard the judge. If I deem a raising necessary to prove cause of death, you're good to go."

Maybe so, but I still wasn't feeling it.

Doc tossed his hands in the air. "Look, the DA's up for reelection. He's a conservative hardliner who jacked you around to court the liberal voters. He made his point. He isn't going to open this can of worms again."

Doc was probably right, but I was the one in the crosshairs. On the other hand, we were crapping out on the Henry murder. If there was even a remote chance that this Vega character was involved somehow, we needed to know. Damn it. Why hadn't Opie been available when I called? In the end, I shouted down the brain bitch and signed off on the agreement, praying this spineless ME had enough intestinal fortitude to stand behind it.

With a copy of the signed document shoved securely into my pocket, I followed Doc, Cap and Harry down the hall to the morgue. It wasn't surprising to see Doc's tables full. Morgues all over the country were overflowing thanks to the heroin and fentanyl epidemics, not to mention the usual spates of natural deaths and homicides. Three steel autopsy tables filled the primary chamber with cold storage drawers lining the far wall. A walk-in freezer at the rear of the room provided additional space for cadaver storage. Doc's attendant glanced up from loading the autoclave and nodded as we walked through the door.

My breath billowed out in a frosty plume as Doc guided us to Vega's body. The ME's office kept the morgue at an even forty degrees to slow decomposition. Doc strolled to the middle table and pulled back the crisp white sheet, uncovering the body of Alejandro Vega. A collective gasp rose through the room.

A gaping slash in the corpse's throat smiled up at us. Amid the gore glistened a tantalizing bit of white. Vega's vertebrae. C_1 or possibly C_2.

I glanced at Doc. "Could the elevator cables have done that?"

Doc shrugged. "Normally, no. Those cables are a twist of

steel wire, coated to protect them from wear and tear. But the building was abandoned for a while. The cable lubricant is long gone. With vermin gnawing on them, and no one servicing the elevator, who knows? There's a lot of metal in the bottom of those shafts, too. He may have fallen in the dark and landed just right, or just wrong, depending on your view. It's also possible someone might have done a Sweeney Todd on him. Gave him the old Columbian necktie. That's what we need to find out."

Long salt and pepper curls corkscrewed around our vic's face, framing a scraggly, predominantly gray goatee. He had chiseled features, pocked translucent cheeks, and a thin-set mouth. Dead isn't an attractive look for anyone, but Vega's face radiated something akin to harshness. Couldn't blame him really. Nobody wants to go out like that.

"Who was this guy?" I asked. "What do we know about him?"

"He's in the system," Doc said, pulling up Vega's record. "A low-level thug, busted several times, mostly for petty shit. But he also served a ten-year stretch at Huntsville for drug trafficking."

"Anything violent?"

Doc checked his file. "He had a few scuffles in the joint. Put one guy in the infirmary with a shiv in his side. Why?"

"Because if he was a mean ass mother in life, he ain't coming back with a smile on his face singing *Sweet Caroline*. He's going to have a ginormous 'tude. Actually," I said, frowning at the wad of shredded pulp that used to be his throat. "He isn't going to be singing anything. Or talking. He'll have to write his answers down on a pad of paper."

Harry snorted. "Can zombies write?"

"Hell if I know. You got a better idea?"

"I'm way ahead of you," Doc said, pointing out twin rows of

tiny sutures deep inside the wound. "I sewed his vocal cords back together for you."

A perfect solution, assuming it worked. So why was I still feeling five kinds of hinky about raising the guy? I gave Doc a chance to change his mind.

"Are you sure you want to do this? Vega is a freshie. Raising a recently deceased corpse is...unpredictable. Bad things can happen."

Doc stared at me like I had three heads. "You, Harry and Cap are all armed. If the damn thing gets feisty, just take it down."

Spoken like someone who'd never seen a raising go south.

"Fine by me, Doc. Just don't say I didn't warn you."

I centered myself, placed my hands over Vega's body, and summoned the preternatural power that would deliver him from the world of the dead. The searing heat in my palms morphed into energy and arced from me into Vega.

"Alejandro Vega, in the name of God, I command you to rise."

His lips curved, forming a nearly imperceptible grin, but otherwise, he remained still. A grin. That was something new. The dead are seldom amused at being awakened. Confused? Yes. Disoriented? Absolutely. But amused? Little Allie was curiously unsettled. So was I.

Closing my eyes, I breathed deep and held the air in my lungs, letting it oxygenate me, cell by cell. When I couldn't hold my breath any longer, I exhaled, opened my eyes and tried again.

"Rise, Alejandro!"

His eyes fluttered open. The subtle curve of his lips remained, giving him an oddly relaxed look, as if I'd just awakened him from a nap.

"I'm going to ask you some questions, Alejandro. You need to answer them as best you can."

He grunted and sat upright, causing his head to flop back and double-dribble against his shoulder blades. His body faced me, but his head faced the wall behind him. I moved to the rear of the autopsy table into his line of sight. He was looking at me upside down. This was the most bizarre raising I'd ever done.

"Alejandro, why were you at The Crosley Building last night?"

A string of guttural grunts and groans gurgled from his neck. Apparently, when Vega's head flopped back, Doc's stitches had given way.

Perfect.

As if the whole shit-show hadn't been challenging enough, Vega did the one thing I prayed he wouldn't do. He twitched. Hand to God, folks, I always end up with the twitchers. It's like they chat me up on their Dead Web Facebook group.

"Retreat. Retreat," I yelled, motioning for everyone to get out while they still had the chance. "Biter blowout imminent. Repeat: Biter blow out imminent."

The morgue attendant screamed and broke for the door, knocking the autoclave to the floor. Her exit was blocked by DA Farragut and two police officers who had just arrived on the scene.

"Arrest that woman," Farragut ordered, pointing to me.

Vega sprang from the table and landed on his feet, whipping his body upright. His barely-connected bobblehead bounced against his shoulder blades, severing the tenuous connection between his skull and spine. His body crumpled into a twitching heap at the foot of the autopsy table, while his head did a double summersault, landing face-up at the morgue attendant's feet. She fainted on cue, like one of those little baby goats.

Vega's head rolled toward the DA like a bowling ball, gnashing its teeth and making wet, sucking noises as the pulpy flesh of its throat slapped against the floor. When Farragut pony-stepped sideways, the head purposely followed him. The bastard was making a run at my least favorite DA. For two cents, I would have let the roly-poly rotterhead have at him, but the brain bitch would have imploded.

I played follow the bouncing head, pulled my 9mm and fired a single round of ballistic therapy into Vega's brain, splattering gray matter across the morgue in an angry arc. That's when I noticed Opie in the doorway, eyes wide and mouth agape.

"What?" I asked, holstering Hawk. "Nobody likes ankle biters. Right?"

Cap, Doc and Harry, Opie, the DA and his minions all stared past me in silent disbelief.

I glanced over my shoulder. Vega's still failing body was floundering on the floor like a beached fish.

What the actual fuck?

"That's not supposed to happen, is it?" Harry muttered.

"I...No that's not supposed to happen!"

Harry shrugged. "Maybe he's like one of those headless chickens, flopping around, after it gets...you know."

Vega's body pinwheeled on the white tile floor like an undead breakdancer. Somehow, despite my head shot, his brain stem was still intact. I drew Hawk and brought him to bear.

It's not easy shooting a pinwheeling, breakdancing deadhead directly in the apricot. It took me six shots to nail the 2.5-centimeter target at the very top of his neck. And with every squeeze of my trigger, more of Vega's tissue splattered the room.

Doc, saucer-eyed and slack jawed, scanned the carnage. His cheeks blazed. His breath came in jagged bursts. The formerly immaculate morgue would require massive doses of biohazard remediation before he could get his operation up and running again.

That was his problem. I told him raising a freshie was unpredictable. He needed to man up and embrace the suckage.

Ignoring Doc's meltdown, Cap reached into his pocket and produced Vega's evidence bag. He held its contents out for the rest of us to see: three grand and a truck rental receipt from Hebron, Kentucky. "I'll bet the bastard drove to tent city and rousted some rotters, baited them into the truck, and then deposited them in the warehouse."

Harry nodded. "That would explain the horde. But who had paid Vega and why?

Good question.

Talk about screwing the pooch. Surrounded by a headless corpse and a corpse-less head, we had no more information now, than when we'd started the raising. The only thing we did have was the change in Doc's attitude. He roused his trauma-tized attendant from the floor, then inspected the trail of zushi slathered across his operating theater, courtesy of seven 9mm bullets and Vega's bowling ball head. Doc's face instantly morphed from royally pissed red to fuck-you fuchsia. I girded my loins for the tirade coming my way in four, three, two, one —

"Never again, Nighthawk. You hear me? Never again. Not in my morgue. Look what you did! You—"

"You asked me to, Doc. You called me and specifically asked me to come here and raise—"

"I was backlogged as it was. If the press finds out about this, they'll have a field day."

Cap and Harry pulled me out the morgue with Doc's rant following us like a rancid fart down the hallway. I hadn't known Doc very long, but I got the distinct impression he didn't like me much.

I can't imagine why.

Farragut followed me into the hallway and shoved his finger in my face. "You should have quit while you were ahead, Ms. Nighthawk. That's two corpses you've raised without the consent of the DA's office."

"Not true," Opie said, exiting the morgue on Farragut's heels. Opie handed our notarized agreement to the DA and did his best to look intimidating. "We got our authorization, sir. We just went around you to get it."

"That's a dangerous game, Mr. Andrews."

"Not as dangerous as sticking your finger near my mouth." I snapped my teeth and slapped Farragut's hand away from my face.

Farragut's eyes turned icy. "Careful, body snatcher. I've got a nasty bite myself."

Convinced that I'd ~~caused, created~~ seen enough mayhem for one day, I turned on my heel and headed out the door to the parking lot for a breath of fresh air.

Big mistake.

16

RUN THIS UP THE OLD FLAGPOLE

No sooner did I hit the sidewalk than Jade Chen rushed me, microphone in hand, and wallpapered herself to my hip. "Miss Nighthawk, is it true you raised yet another corpse without securing a court order?"

Freaking news floozy. "No. In fact, it is not true."

"But our sources—"

"Yeah? Well. Your sources suck rocks," I said, resisting the urge to cram the microphone down her tiny, perfect throat.

Opie pushed through the doors behind me and stepped into the melee, making a beeline for Jade. "Ms. Chen, I'll be answering your questions today."

The media hive swarmed Opie, leaving me behind faster than yesterday's sushi.

Harry strolled alongside me and whispered, "I've never met a real, live cadaver diver before. Can I have your autograph?"

"Bite me, Harry." We walked to the parking lot in silence, listening to Opie finesse the media. "He's not half bad," I said.

"Especially since he's free." Harry opened the door to his Crown Vic and ducked inside. "I'm headed back to the office to check out Veronica's phone records and bank balances. You working tonight?"

"Six to closing," I said, peering into his passenger window. "Got a couple Guinness's with your name on them. See you then?"

"It's almost like you know me, partner."

I left the morgue feeling proud of myself. It was only one o'clock, and I had successfully alienated two asshats who considered themselves my superiors: Doc hated my guts and Farragut wanted me in jail. With all the excitement, I'd forgotten to check in with Cap. I hadn't earned a place on his shit list yet, but given my track record with authority figures, it was only a matter of time.

I shifted my Lowrider into neutral, coasted up the driveway, and waved across the yard at Mrs. Nussbaum, not because I could see her peering out from behind her curtains but because I could feel her there. The last thing I wanted to deal with was another skirmish in the Battle of the Bushes. When I slid my key into the back door, it drifted open.

I froze at the threshold and glanced around the kitchen. Nothing seemed out of place.

Little Allie whispered, *Where's Headbutt?*

True to form, he was lying on the register vent, snoring. Snoring deeper than I'd ever heard him, with an empty burger wrapper inches from his nose.

The hair on the back of my neck prickled. I slid Hawk from his holster, took a step inside and whispered, "Headbutt?"

No answer. That dog may have been kinetically challenged, but there was nothing wrong with his hearing. Asleep or not, he would have roused at the sound of the door, let alone my voice. His snores stopped. I watched his chest, hoping to see it fall or rise. It didn't. I scrambled to his side, took his head in my hands, and whispered his name. And then the world went dark.

"Mrs. Nighthawk? Mrs. Nighthawk?" A resounding *crack* pealed in my ears. The side of my face blazed. I opened my eyes to find Mrs. Nussbaum pulling her arm back to deliver another slap. Even semiconscious, I was fast enough to grab her hand and stop her from making the biggest mistake of her life. For future reference, slapping someone in the face to wake them up after they've been knocked unconscious is a poor choice.

"Mrs. Nighthawk? Are you all right? Mrs. Nighthawk?"

Oh, my freaking head. I rolled onto my side and tried to sit up. A wave of nausea washed over me and sent me crashing face-first to the floor. *Headbutt.* "Where's Headbutt?"

"Big ugly golem right here."

The smell of dog breath wafted up my nose and a large wet tongue slurped the side of my face. I opened my eyes and sighed. "You okay, boy?"

"He seem to be." Mrs. Nussbaum wrapped one arm beneath my shoulders and helped me sit up. "He wobbly when I get here, like too much whiskey. Better now."

"What happened?"

"Earlier, I just happens to see man on your porch…"

"Uh huh." As if she isn't glued to that freaking window watching every move I make.

"Then I see you come home and go inside. Later, I look and back door is open. I come. See you on floor, with dog on top like big furry blanket."

I stumbled to my feet, ignoring the pain in my head. The room whirled a few times before sliding to a halt. My eyes came to rest on the empty burger wrapper. Somebody drugged my dog. That was the only way they'd get inside without losing an appendage. Whoever it was had thrown a tainted burger through the door and waited until Headbutt passed out to break in.

But why? Why break in here? Unless the bastard had a taste for Ramen noodles, he wouldn't find much. I bent over to pick Hawk up off the floor and instantly regretted it. My head throbbed. I opened the cabinet door above the stove and groped for my bottle of Tylenol. A sideways glance into the living room made me moan out loud. The place had been tossed.

Mrs. Nussbaum clucked behind me like a mother hen. "You call police. Yes?"

"Absolutely. You bet." I walked her to the back door, silently inviting her to leave. "Thank you for coming, Mrs. Nussbaum. But in the future, if you think I'm in trouble, you should lock your doors and call the police. If anyone had still been in the house, you could have been hurt today."

She gave me a worried smile, and as she waddled across the yard to her house, I wondered how I knew for sure that someone else wasn't still in the house. I hadn't cleared it.

Hawk drawn and at high ready, I moved from room to room, double checking my stash of munitions and ~~napalm~~ 'golf balls.' Thankfully, they were still locked safely away. Headbutt and I were alone — alone with all our questions. Who broke in? And why? Was it just my luck or was I being targeted? I called Harry and told him about the break in. He said he was on his way, which gave me twenty minutes for a quick shower before he arrived.

I slipped beneath the hot water and let it pulse against my skin, washing away the bio-chum from the earlier raising (which seemed like days ago), soothing the tension from my neck, and dulling the ache in my head. I didn't want to get out. But I needed to get dressed. I walked to my closet and pulled out some clean jeans, giving Headbutt a kiss along the way. He'd scared the crap out of me. Covered me like a big furry blanket, did he? He was protecting me. I don't know why I was surprised. He was a hell of a zombie hunter. And I'd have done the same for him.

———

Harry's knees creaked as he squatted to pet Headbutt. "Somebody slipped you a mickey, fella. Gotta keep your head in the game. Don't let it happen again. *Capiche?*"

Headbutt lowered his head, slunk to his register vent and plopped into napping position.

Harry turned his attention to me. "How's your head?"

I ran my fingers across the walnut-sized lump on the back of my skull and winced. "I'll live. Thanks for asking."

A couple of detectives wandered through my house checking for prints and trace evidence. They were none too happy that I'd showered and changed clothes. One of them mumbled something about me "knowing better." He was lucky I wasn't in the mood to dance. I picked up my dirty, zushi-stained clothes, threw them at the officers, and watched them recoil in disgust. One of them stuffed the clothes into an evidence bag and I groaned. Great. One more set of clothes donated to the black hole, otherwise known as the evidence room. An industrial hazard in my line of work.

I scooped up the rest of my dirty clothes and mounded them into a pile to create a path for Harry. He toured the house, room by room, and asked several times if anything was missing. There wasn't.

"Who knows?" I said. "Probably just some crackhead looking for something to fence."

"Maybe." Harry's tone sounded like he wasn't buying my theory. "What if...we've been looking at the case all wrong?

Maybe we aren't the only ones who know about Veronica's book. Maybe the killer does too."

I paused, letting that sink in.

"You know," Harry continued, "if you're right about that book being a ledger, with a lot of important names inside, maybe the killer suspects that you found it. But instead of turning it in, you decided to play fast and loose. Make a little money, shake somebody down. It's no secret you're working the case. It's all over the media."

The lightbulb in my head came on. "Then every name in that book is a potential suspect — for both the killing and the break in."

We took a couple of moments to run this theory up the old flagpole and see how it shook out.

Harry finally said, "There is one other angle to consider. Maybe this little visit was a message telling you to back off the investigation. Better grow eyes in the back of your head."

Yet another unsettling theory. I'd had enough of running things up the old flagpole for one day.

The detectives were nearly finished collecting evidence. Their next stop would be to chat with Mrs. Nussbaum. God bless them. Harry had to finish Veronica's records review back at the office. He said his goodbyes and moseyed down the side-walk, scribbling something in his notebook. With a wave, he sunk into the Crown Vic and disappeared behind the glare of the afternoon sun. It was new, this having a partner thing. New but nice. He worried for me. And I worried for him.

"Watch your six," I murmured, as he drove down the street.

I had the next couple of hours to do laundry before reporting to work at The Blue Note. The only one with nothing on his agenda was Headbutt. I gave him a pass. Taking care of me is a 24/7 job and today, he'd come through like a champ.

17

NEVER WALK AWAY

The Blue Note was jumping when I walked through the door. Between the yapping, laughing, and wailing juke box, the crowd sounded entirely too happy. I cursed my throbbing head and tossed back more Tylenol, telling myself that the crowd was a good thing. More people, more tips. As long as I didn't kill anyone before the night was over. The odds were still out on that.

Dallas moved behind the bar to serve Jimmy, Hank and the other regulars, while I worked the floor. Some tables turned over quickly, while others ordered food and round after round of drinks. One table, louder than the others, ran me ragged. A six-top filled with eight crazy chicks who drank their weight in vodka, swore like sailors, and greeted each new member by screaming, "Hey, Bitch!"

The front door opened, letting in a blast of cold January air. I was bussing tables and didn't notice who'd come in. I'd hoped it was Harry, and realized for the first time that he was later than usual.

The hair on the back of my neck stood up as a collective chant filled the room.

"Stretch! Stretch! Stretch!"

I spun on my heel and caught sight of Tiffany Swarovski navigating the crowd, and heading for the six-top of crazy bitches. The conversation Harry and I had with the late Veronica Henry looped through my brain. We'd asked if she knew who'd killed her, and she'd answered, "Find book." And when we asked where her book was, she'd answered, "Stretch."

After all this time...could *Stretch* be a person? And could that person be Tiffany Swarovski? I slid the tub of dirty dishes down the bar and made a beeline for Tiffany.

"Hey, girlfriend," she said, sweeping her hand before her posse. "I see you've met my bitches. Ladies, this is Nighthawk."

I narrowed my eyes. "Your friends call you Stretch?"

"My...business associates do. Why?"

Tiffany and Veronica, two working girls, albeit different clientele. What were the odds?

"Excuse us, bitches," I said, taking Tiffany's arm. "We'll be right back."

I dragged Tiffany through the kitchen to the back door, drawing a dubious stare from Dallas.

"We're going out back for a smoke break," I yelled.

"You don't smoke."

"I do now." I yanked Tiffany out the door. "Spill it, Stretch."

"Spill what?"

Wearing her snakeskin stilettos, she had a good six inches on me. No wonder they called her Stretch. She pushed against me, trying to get away, as if she had something to hide. Little Allie wanted to know what; so did I.

I grabbed her coat collar and shoved her against the dumpster, hard. "Why didn't you tell me you knew Veronica Henry?"

"You never asked. Damn, girl. That hurt." She squinted down her nose at me. "How you know Veronica?"

"Harry and I are working her murder investigation with CPD."

"But…you work here."

"I work with Harry, too. It's complicated. Where's her book?"

"What book?"

"The book you're holding for her."

"You trippin', girl. I ain't holding no book."

"She gave it to you for safekeeping."

"Ha! Fat chance. Everybody know ain't nothin' safe with me."

She darted her eyes searching for an escape. Had I actually scared her? That didn't seem likely. "You aren't in trouble for having the book. I just need you to give it to me. That's all. Or I can call the CPD and get a couple of uniforms here."

"Shit. I don't want the dang thing anyway. Just having it gives me nine kinds of agita."

"What's inside it?"

"Hell if I know." Tiffany shrugged and looked away. "And I don't want to know neither. She called it her *insurance*. That girl had some high-powered clients, she did. Don't want nothing to do with them."

Dallas would be out any minute hunting for me. I needed to wrap up this little heart-to-heart. "Go back inside and party with your bitch buddies. Just don't tell anyone about our conversation. Hang onto that book. For now, keep it wherever the hell you hid it. And bring it here tomorrow morning at eleven."

Tiffany let her bitch flag fly. "Who you think you are, ho? You and those tiny-ass midget hands of yours, all up in my face. I'll squash you like a bug. Thinking you can tell me what to—"

"Tiffany?"

"*What?*"

"Bring me the book."

"Fine. But you screwed up my shoulder blades, slamming me against that dumpster. I feel a big ol' knot coming on.

Prolly knocked my discuses all outta whack. I might have to sue."

Holy hell. That was all I needed. "How about a Tequila Sunrise instead? On the house."

"Double? Three cherries, light ice. Heavy on the grenadine."

"You got it, girlfriend."

"Okay. We cool. But don't be putting those itty-bitty midget hands on me again, Imma snap you like a twig."

* * *

I ushered Tiffany inside, scanned the entire bar, and frowned. Nine o'clock and still no sign of Harry. Before Dallas caught sight of me, I ducked into the restroom, whipped out my phone, and dialed Harry's number.

My voice went up two octaves when he answered. "Where the hell are you?"

"Sorry. It was getting late, so I brought the records home. Still at it. But I think I figured out who our killer is. You are never going to believe it."

"Who?"

"Not on the phone. If I'm right, our ah...*circle of trust* just got a lot smaller."

"No shit? I've got some news for you, too." Based on Harry's warning, I thought twice about blurting it out.

"Save it," he said. "Meet you at the bar at closing time. You can tell me then."

* * *

The night stayed busy, but closing time couldn't arrive fast enough. I needed to get the hell out of there. The case was breaking wide open, while I was serving drinks, mopping floors and rolling silverware. Eventually, the crowd thinned out. Dallas sent Jimmy packing after he knocked over one too many beers. Hank cashed out behind him. Tiffany and her bitches took their party elsewhere, but not before I caught her eye and mouthed the words "eleven o'clock." She rolled her eyes and nodded on her way out the door.

When 2:30 a.m. rolled around, Dallas turned off the neon *Open* sign and counted out my pay for the night. "Here's an extra ten. Help cover that new smoking habit of yours."

I shoved the money into my pocket, snapped on my knife sheath, and slipped on my holster while Dallas punched in the alarm code.

"See you tomorrow, say five o'clock? It's Friday. Going to make tonight seem like a test run."

I slipped into my duster and told him I'd be there. We turned off the lights and closed the door behind us.

Still no sign of Harry.

Dallas offered me a ride but I waved him off and started my Harley, cranking up the heated seat and hand grips.

"Come on, Harry," I thought. *"It's cold out here."*

I looked at my phone and sighed. No missed calls, no messages. That wasn't like Harry. But he was a cop, and he was really wrapped up in those records. He was probably just running late. I dialed his number. The call went straight to voice mail.

Little Allie wheedled me. *Something's wrong.* But she's such a freaking drama queen. I waited a couple of minutes, then counted to ten and hit redial.

"You have reached the voice mail of Detective Harry Delk—"

Listen to me! The brain bitch shouted. *Something is fucking WRONG.*

Winter wind be damned, I tore up the expressway, making the twenty-minute drive to Harry's place in ten flat. I cut my engine at the top of his street and coasted to the end of his driveway. A silence, thick and stagnant, draped his house — the kind of silence that churns in your gut. The kind that shoots bile up your throat when you realize how very wrong things are.

A faint light shone from deep in the house. The garage door was closed, the living room curtains drawn. As I crept through the darkness to Harry's porch, nothing looked out of place. But that's what darkness does. It camouflages wrong. *Everything's fine*, it soothes. *Nothing to see here. Move along.*

Fuck that.

My gift and I know darkness better than anyone. We do and see what should never be in our line of work every single day. We understand that no matter how ugly it gets you never turn your back and walk away. I grabbed the knob and sucked in a breath as the door to Harry Delk's house popped open.

18

NO, NO, NO

I drew Hawk, raised him to high ready, and stepped across the threshold. "Harry?" His name came out in a whisper. I called again, louder. "Harry. It's Nighthawk."

Frantic fluttering filled the air, followed by a piercing screech.

"Help me! Help me!"

What the hell? ... Holy shit. That cry hadn't come from Harry. It'd come from his bird.

I pulled out my phone, turned on the flashlight and pushed deeper into the house, clearing each room along the way. Trusting my sight was risky. The street light cast shadows on the walls, painting boogeymen that faded before my very eyes. I used all my senses, feeling the rooms, absorbing their energy. Smells provided context for what I couldn't see. The sweet scents of millet, seeds and fruit, the tang of tomatoes, no, not just tomatoes, seasonings too. Marinara sauce. Traces of oil and gunpowder teased my nose.

Not to worry, I told myself. *Harry's been cleaning his .38.*

A few feet later, I rounded the corner into the kitchen. A

sickening odor emerged, cloying, metallic and all too familiar. *No, no, no —*

I slipped in something slick and fell face first to the floor. Swallowing back the vomit in my throat, I shined my flashlight along the outline of a body. A mewling sound escaped me as I staggered to my feet and slid my hand along the wall in search of a light switch. With a flick of a finger, Harry's body came into view. The top of his head was missing. Some of it clung to the crevices of the popcorn ceiling, the rest sprayed Warhol-style across the room.

A quick scan found his .38, snug in its holster, draped across the back of a kitchen chair. The brain bitch slapped me hard, snapping me back into tactical mode. *Harry hadn't seen this coming.* She was right. But there was something else. Whoever did this made sure Harry couldn't be raised to help me nail his killer.

Cap needed to know, but Harry's voice rang in my ear, reminding me that our *"circle of trust"* had shrunk. I ran a quick search on Harry's computer for Veronica Henry's records and came up empty, so I hunted for a flash drive (apologizing profusely to Harry as I rummaged through his pockets). Printed copies seemed unlikely, but I scoured the place anyway, rifling through things, using a paper towel in lieu of my fingers.

Snake eyes. Zilch. Zip. Nada.

Unless CPD's tech guys could find what I had not, those records were missing in action, i.e. stolen. Sure, they could be reproduced but that would take some time. Time we didn't have. I couldn't put it off any longer. I needed to call it in. Little Allie argued with me, reasoning that too many hands would lead to a tainted investigation. She might have been right, but what choice did I have? After taking a moment to collect myself, I called Cap and gave voice to a fact I hadn't fully processed.

"Harry Delk's been murdered."

Cap, Doc and the forensic investigative team arrived within the hour. I lingered in the dining room, on the periphery of the immediate crime scene, watching the professionals do what they do best, and wondering if any of their names were in Veronica's book.

Once Cap officially cleared the second floor, I walked up the steps, leaving the fray behind, and found a bathroom where I could clean myself up. My clothes, hands and hair were drenched in Harry's blood. I needed to change, but I didn't have a set of clothes with me. His pants would never fit. Harry had 125 pounds on me. I washed up as best I could, then rummaged through his drawers in search of a clean shirt. The winner was a black T-shirt plastered with the picture of a smoking .38, bearing the slogan *Ballistic Therapy*. I snickered and slipped it over my head. It hung to my knees. Wrapping the excess folds around me, I closed my eyes and pictured Harry wearing the cotton tee. I knew in my heart it was a keeper. I didn't think he would mind.

After a few deep breaths, I returned to the first floor. Cap wanted to know why I was there. I told him about Harry's call, and that he thought he'd found Veronica's killer. Cap ran me through the course of my evening several times, an old investigative technique designed to do two things: either shred holes in a perpetrator's version of events, or secure additional facts a stressed-out witness might have forgotten.

Standard operating procedure? Maybe, but it was insulting. And it pissed me off. I'm a corpse whisperer, damn it. My life is the definition of high stress. I'll never have the luxury of forgetting a single moment of that night. But that wasn't all that was bothering me.

Questions about the timeline made me uneasy. I'd delayed reporting Harry's murder to search for Veronica Henry's records. Not only did I not have the records, I had to play fast and loose when accounting for my time. I debated whether to tell Cap that Harry had been working on Veronica's records at home that night and finally decided there was no way around it. Those records had been booked into evidence and now they were missing.

The forensic guys collected evidence and took samples of my hair and DNA for exclusionary purposes. Doc quietly escorted Harry's body away around daybreak. By the time the last of the investigators left, 9 a.m. had come and gone.

I couldn't bring myself to leave.

Cap hung back with me. I'd like to believe that he stayed to be supportive, but we both knew, by law, as a material witness, I couldn't be left unattended at the crime scene. Harry's bird scrambled back and forth on its perch, craning its neck, and calling Harry's name. Poor thing. Who would care for it now that Harry was gone?

What was its name? Lulu? Sulu?

I wandered over to its cage, dumped the cup of empty seed husks, and pulled a bag of bird seed from a box that contained a book titled *Your African Grey Parrot* and some other bird-related crap. The box was labeled "Kulu."

That's right. Kulu.

My tears fell fast and embarrassingly hard. Stupid tears. There's no crying in corpse whispering.

"Harry's dead," I whispered to that silly bird.

Harry, the self-professed dinosaur, who carried not one but two .38s — who could hunt Zs with the best of the best. The only partner I ever had worth his salt. The only partner I'd ever liked. Who'd bailed my ass out of jail, hooked me up with an attorney, and even cared for my dog when I couldn't.

I hadn't known him long, but Harry had been my friend.

I reached inside the cage to replace the freshly filled seed cup and Kulu, the parrot who sings "Drunk on a Plane," bit the shit out of my finger and told me to fuck off.

"Strike One, Birdzilla." I slammed the cage door closed and carried it to the front door, mumbling the entire way.

Cap followed, lugging the box of assorted bird crap. When he locked the door behind us, it occurred to me that I would never see Harry again. And neither would Kulu. As we ducked beneath the yellow crime scene tape, I turned her cage away from the house so she wouldn't realize she was leaving.

Picturing her strapped to the back of my Harley, losing her feathers at sixty mph snapped me into my new reality. "Cap, would you mind hauling the bird to my house?"

He nodded and took the cage, silently depositing it into his back seat

Just like that, without a moment's deliberation, I'd become a foster parent for a foul-mouthed, finger-eating bird. I didn't have enough dog biscuits to feed Headbutt or me, let alone that flying feather duster.

What the hell was I thinking?

19

DISTURBING VISUALS

Since Cap was following me to my place, I made an executive decision to not cut the engine of my Harley and coast down the street to my house. Screw Mrs. Nussbaum. It would be hard to explain to Cap, and frankly, a little embarrassing. I gunned it up the driveway, sprinted to the porch, and unlocked the house. Then I ran back to Cap's car to grab the box of bird seed while he carried Kulu to the door. Once we got inside, Headbutt eyed us warily from his throne on the heat vent.

"Thanks for taking care of the bird," he said, setting the cage on my kitchen table. "I'll contact Harry's next of kin when I get to the office. I'm sure they'll take her off your hands."

He turned toward me and caught my eye. "Why don't you take the rest of the day off. Get some sleep. Stop in my office tomorrow around noon. We can chat then."

He bent down and peered into the cage, sticking his finger through the bars. "Cute little thing, isn't she?"

Kulu puffed up like a blowfish and grew to twice her size. It might have been my tired eyes, but she did a little shimmy that sort of resembled...a twitch. She reminded me of one of those acid-spitting dinosaurs from Jurassic Park. "Cap, I wouldn't—"

That little shit clamped down on Cap's finger like a vice grip. The more he flailed, the harder she bit. I slapped the side of the cage, drawing Kulu's attention. She let Cap go, ruffled her feathers, then turned her head sideways and gave me the stink eye.

Cap ripped his bleeding finger out of the cage and stomped his foot. "Mother Fu—"

"Yes. Yes, she is."

He pulled out his handkerchief to wrap the wound. "Did you see that? That twitching bastard took a chunk out of my finger."

"Fucking twitchers," I said, shaking my head. "Get you every time."

———

Four, three, two, one. Mrs. Nussbaum was on my porch before Cap even cleared the driveway.

"Crazy bitch," I mumbled, throwing the door open.

"Who dat man?" she asked, poking her head through the doorway. Her nosey eyes scoured the kitchen, then landed on Kulu and narrowed. "What *dat*?"

"A parrot. Mrs. Nussbaum this is Kulu. Kulu this is—"

"Crazy bitch! Crazy bitch!"

Note to self: this is one smart bird.

"Sorry. I'm pet-sitting for a friend. This isn't a good time. I need to be somewhere. I'll try to teach Kulu some manners."

"Who teach *you* first, eh?"

I closed the door in her face.

I might have been rude, but I hadn't been lying. Come eleven o'clock, Tiffany Swarovski would be waiting for me at The Blue Note with Veronica's mystery book. After a quick shower, I checked Kulu's seed and water, and shared a few dog biscuits with Headbutt. He glared at Kulu as if he expected her to swoop down and snarf his treat. Headbutt's no dummy. It was only a matter of time before Birdzilla stepped up to vie for pack leader. I checked the latch on her cage door and let Headbutt out to pee, praying Mrs. Nussbaum had had her fill of abuse for one day and wouldn't be lying in wait behind her window, hoping to catch Headbutt in the act of *rosebush urinationus.*

When she didn't fly out the door brandishing a flyswatter and threatening to whap Headbutt, I couldn't help feel a bit disappointed. Little Allie pecked at me. *Maybe you hurt the gum grinder's feelings. Maybe your manners suck. In fact, maybe they suck like a five-dollar whore.*

Seriously, people?

That stupid brain bitch, always filling my head with namby-pamby, touchy-feely bullshit. I coasted down the driveway and kept the noise to a minimum until I hit the stop sign. Then I gunned it toward The Blue Note and told that *holier than thou* head hag to kiss my ass.

<hr>

The vacuum droned out of sight as I walked into The Blue Note. Dallas had beaten me there, but Tiffany had yet to arrive. It was a good time to tell Dallas about Harry. When I finished the story, Dallas slid onto a bar stool and ran his hands through his hair.

"Damn, Allie," was all he could manage.

He poured us both a shot of Maker's.

"To Harry," he said.

"To Harry." I tossed back the smooth, sweet bourbon and sighed.

Dallas reached for the bottle.

"Not for me, thanks," I said, putting my hand over my glass. Things were heating up. I needed to keep my head clear. "Listen, I'm meeting Tiffany here in a few minutes. I know she and Harry were close, but let's keep the news about Harry between us for now."

On cue, Tiffany Swarovski burst through the door, wearing a spotted, faux-fur trench coat with matching head scarf, hot pink sunglasses, and five-inch black patent leather heels.

I stifled a laugh. "Nice outfit, Cruella."

"I'm going incogro...incongo... I'm whatchacallit. Flying under the radar." She reached into her purse, pulled out a worn black book, and slid it across the bar. "There. Happy?"

"Ecstatic." I picked it up and shoved it into the breast pocket in my duster, still staring at her ensemble. "Not that I'm an expert, but aren't you a little overdressed for this hour of the day?"

"How the hell should I know?" she wailed. "Only times I'm up this early, I'm in jail, wearing what I wore the night before. Who picked this time to meet, anyway?" She turned toward Dallas, batted her eyes and threw him a kiss. "Later, baby. You and me."

He grinned as she sauntered out the door, looking like a perfectly accessorized six-foot Dalmatian. The door closed with a thud, leaving Dallas with nothing but a dream.

"Wouldn't that be something?" he said wistfully, wiping down the bar. "I'm not sure I'd survive, but I wouldn't mind giving it a shot."

Talk about a disturbing visual. That was my cue to leave. I had work to do.

"See you at five," I said, slipping off my stool and heading for the door.

"No. Take some time. You and Harry were close. You don't need to be here."

"It's fine," I said, waving him off. "Friday's are busy. That's a good thing. It'll keep me occupied."

The door closed behind me before he had a chance to argue. I hopped on my Harley, tore up the streets and headed for home. Veronica Henry's mystery book awaited.

I was so happy to finally get a look at that little black book, that I cut Mrs. Nussbaum some slack and coasted up my driveway. The good karma instantly paid off. Her face wasn't peering out the window, and I had a shot at reaching the door before she discovered I was home.

Little Allie went to Defcon 2 when my feet hit the porch. Things were much too quiet. No barking, growling, or screeching (from Headbutt, Kulu or Mrs. Nussbaum). After a quick turn of the key, I stepped inside and scanned the room. Headbutt, lounging on his vent, opened one bloodshot eye to acknowledge my presence. Kulu, puffed like a toad, sulked on her perch with her eyes closed, probably strategizing an aerial attack for when I let her out of her cage.

Like that would ever happen.

After a quick cup of ramen, I settled onto the couch to read Veronica's best kept secrets. The small, leather-bound book measured six by four and was a good inch thick, filled with page after page of data, including notations in the margins. Veronica had scribbled like a farsighted chipmunk, making most of the entries illegible. But a closer look revealed the real problem. The book was written in cipher.

It made sense that a high-priced hooker like Veronica would document her transactions. If one of her elite clients ever decided she was a liability, she had an ace in the hole. And what better way to protect that ace than to encrypt it in code? Smart chick, this Veronica Henry. So where was the key?

I could have studied that book 'til The Rapture and never broken the code. But I wasn't ready to ask for help. Harry was right about playing this close to the vest. Every power mogul noted in that book was a potential suspect. Two questions came to mind: How many of those big shots knew about the book's existence? And of those, how many were willing to kill to keep it from going public?

Kulu's seed cup crashed to the floor of the cage, breaking my concentration. She beat her wings defiantly, knocking her swing off its hooks.

"Flappy bastard," I mumbled, approaching her with an abundance of caution.

Empty seed husks littered the floor of the cage. *Crap.* She was hungry.

"Back up, Birdzilla."

She puffed, turned her head and stared, daring me to make my move.

"Chillax, Kulu." I opened the cage door and advanced slowly, fingers low, palm facing away from her.

She lunged half-heartedly but let me remove the cup.

After filling it with fresh seed, I returned it to its holder, then slowly withdrew my hand. She even let me put her swing back up. No bites. No blood. Progress.

"Thank you, Kulu," I whispered.

"You're welcome."

She spoke! ... Something nice! I put the seed back in Kulu's box and reached for the book *Your African Grey Parrot.*

"Harry?" She screeched, swiveling on her perch, turning her head from side to side and scanning the room. "Harry?"

Ah, geez. "I'm Allie. Harry is...gone."

"Gone?"

"Gone."

Kulu moved to the seed cup and chowed while I leafed through the book on parrot care, learning more than I ever wanted to know about their diet, care, and habits. There was even a section on how to know if your parrot is stressed: Fluffing, check. Screeching, check. Aggression, check. Biting, check-check.

"You're not the only one, Kulu," I whispered, snapping the book closed and stretching out across the couch. It had been a long, horrible and heartbreaking day. Sometimes, all you can do is close your eyes and wish it all away.

———

At 4:45 p.m. I put Headbutt in charge and gave him strict instructions not to fuck with the bird. Before slipping out the door, I shoved Veronica's book in my jacket, then made eye contact with Kulu and said goodbye.

She tilted her head and murmured, "Harry?"

"Harry is gone."

"Gone, gone. Harry gone. Bye-bye Harry."

The words didn't want to come. "Yes. Bye-bye Harry." I paused and pointed to myself. "Allie. I am Allie. Say bye-bye Allie."

"Bye-bye Harry Allie."

Close enough.

———

I should have realized that by the time I walked into The Blue Note, all the regulars would have heard the news about Harry. The whole reason I worked that night (other than the money) was to get my mind off him. But in between waiting tables, pouring drinks, and mopping floors, unwanted condolences smacked me in the face, barbed-wire reminders of a loss I wanted...no...needed to put aside if I were ever going to solve this case.

Opie strolled in around eleven, as the crowd began to thin. Tiffany arrived a few minutes later. She strutted to a corner booth and hooked up with some guy who was likely her 'date' for the evening. I took a much-needed break and joined Opie at the bar, only to have him blindside me with another condolence. But this one came with a double shot of Jack from someone who had been a close friend of Harry's. Not to mention, Opie had saved my ass once or twice. I gave him a pass. I poured my double in a cocktail glass, added crushed ice, and made a Jack Daniel's slushie.

"To Harry," Opie said, tossing his back.

"To Harry." A sip of smooth goodness trickled down my throat.

My eardrums almost ruptured at the sound of Jade Chen's voice. "Good evening, Cincinnati. I join officers from the 51st Precinct today in mourning the loss of Detective Harry Delk. Delk, slain in his home overnight, during the early morning hours, was a thirty-year veteran of the Cincinnati Police Force, as well as a close colleague of mine. Captain Philip Dorsey had this to say about Delk..."

I turned away from Opie and stared into Jade Chen's face, splashed across the big screen. The slushie I'd been holding imploded in my hand. Glass, whiskey, blood and ice slipped through my fingers onto the floor.

Opie grabbed my hand. "*Shit*, Nighthawk."

Dallas scrambled for a clean white towel while Opie teased the remaining shards of glass out of my skin.

Tiffany leapt from her booth and roared up beside me. "You bitch! Harry was my friend. Why didn't you tell me he was murdered? Or didn't you think I needed to know, now that you've got what you wanted?" She stomped back to her booth in tears, grabbed her purse, and lit out, leaving her john behind.

Opie stared into his beer. "She's really taking this hard."

"You heard her. They were friends," I said.

But there could have been another reason for her hasty departure. She probably figured she was next. And for all I knew, she could be. Had I dragged Tiffany into harm's way?

"You're lucky," Dallas said, inspecting my hand. "Nothing a few steri-strips and gauze can't fix."

He bandaged my hand and pronounced me cured. As if it were that easy.

I moved behind the bar and poured myself a replacement double. "God, I hate that bitch."

"Tiffany?" Dallas snorted. "She's okay. Just a—"

"No! Jade Chen, damn it. That two-faced media whore. She didn't know Harry. She's using his murder to boost her ratings. Fucking talking head. One of these days, I'm going to reach down her throat, rip out her tongue and—"

Dallas slapped his hand on the bar and nodded at Opie. "Why don't you drive Allie home? I think she's done for the night."

"I'm fine," I said, swallowing my anger.

"No. You aren't. You lost a good friend. Besides, you're no good to me here, bleeding. And those cuts need to clot before you operate that bike. Let Tim take you home." Dallas paid me from the till and shooed me out.

I collected my weapons, threw on my duster and walked my Harley around the back of the bar for safekeeping. Then I slumped into the passenger seat of Tim's Hyundai.

"Thank you." Even as I said it, the words rang angry in my ears.

We passed the ride in awkward silence.

I nearly jumped out of his car when he pulled into my driveway.

Opie opened his door and started to climb out. "Let me walk you in."

"This isn't a freaking date! Goodnight. And...thank you,

again. Even if it doesn't sound sincere." I stomped to the porch, dismissing Opie as if he were nothing more than an Uber driver.

Frantic barks and growls greeted me from the other side of the door.

Chillax, it's just me, boy, I thought, as I slipped the key into the knob and gave it a turn.

A FedEx box tucked against the house caught my eye. I hadn't ordered anything. *Must be Nonnie's,* I figured, scooping it up with my good hand and stepping inside.

Headbutt raced across the kitchen wild-eyed, his face covered with blood.

"Ah, shit," I moaned. "Tell me you didn't eat the bird."

A soft, strange sound drifted in from the living room. Swish thump. Swish thump. Swish thump. The sound repeated, louder. And closer.

Little Allie whispered, *We're not alone.*

Perfect.

My shooting hand had more holes than a block of Swiss cheese. Blood clotted or not, I dropped the FedEx box, ripped off the bandage, and drew Hawk.

Headbutt charged through the archway into the living room with me on his six.

20

BIG OL' ASSHAT

I stopped short and gawked at what was left of my living room. Furniture, toppled and broken, entrails strung across the blood-soaked hardwood. Various internal organs scattered high and low. Wads of zushi, clinging to the walls and ceiling, slowly rained to the floor in random chum bombs and exploded on impact.

One of the bombs splatted onto the roof of Kulu's cage, raising a tortured chorus of, "Help me! Help me!"

I looked at Headbutt and almost spewed. "Put that down!"

A decomped human femur hung from his jaws like an oversized chew toy. The bottom half of the leg lay five feet away. What I assumed to be the matching leg splayed across the staircase. A torso, complete with head, straddled the couch and chattered its teeth at me.

A freaking corpsicle.

Its eyes followed me as I ventured closer, wondering how best to put it down. A bullet to the head seemed anticlimactic, but a blade to the brain meant hands on. No thanks. The living room was already a goner. Adding a headshot to this bloodbath would be like spitting into the ocean.

I brought Hawk to bear and fired, pulverizing the biter's teeth into tiny, fluoride-treated shrapnel.

Opie stood in the doorway, hyperventilating.

I holstered my 9mm, giving him a moment to recover.

He finally blurted, "Is that... Are you okay?"

I scowled at the mess. "Freaking awesome. Didn't I tell you to go home?"

"You're not the boss of me."

I let that slide. It's no fun chasing low-hanging fruit. Remembering the FedEx package, I puddle-jumped the carnage back to the kitchen and ripped the tape off the box. A zombie attack and a mystery delivery on the same day. What were the odds?

Opie eyed my living room and shook his head. "What exactly happened here?"

I lifted a newspaper wrapped parcel from the box and unwrapped it, then hurled its contents to the floor. A dead flounder with a black rose shoved down its throat.

"This?" I motioned from the fish to the zushi-covered battlefield and back again. "This was a message. Someone's telling me to back off."

"Maybe you should."

"Not a chance in hell," I growled. "The fun's just getting started."

I reported the "death" per law. The coroner and a uniform arrived, both looking massively pissed to have been called out at that late hour to verify the cause of death for "a collection of corpsicle chum."

It took some arguing, but Opie finally agreed to drive me back to the bar for my bike on his way home. I assured him that my hand was fine and promised to call if I needed him. But as I pointed out, between Headbutt and me, we had most any situation covered. My zombie hunting bulldog had made one hell of a mess, but he'd disabled that rotter and kept me from walking into a more dangerous situation.

When I got back home, I tossed Headbutt a Bully Stick, then phoned Splatz, my favorite biohazard cleanup company. They'd be at my house by first light.

Flat broke or not, I have limits. I put 'em down. Somebody else cleans 'em up. Besides, with my frequent flyer discount points, I might qualify for a BOGO. In my line of work, messes like this happen more often than you'd think.

Mrs. Nussbaum must have slept through the commotion. Thank God. That's all I needed. One call from Nosey Nonnie and the local HOA vigilantes would drive me out of the neighborhood with torches and pitchforks.

I took a long hot shower, cleaned out the cuts on my hand, then slapped a few Band-Aids back on. Good as new. After throwing my clothes in the washer, I wiped down my leather duster, feeling the outline of Veronica's black book in the breast pocket. I pulled it out. Just to be safe, it was going to spend the night under my pillow.

I let Headbutt out to do his business and watched to make sure he didn't do anything stupid to wake up Mrs. Nussbaum. When he trotted back inside, I gave him a bedtime biscuit. I pulled out an old sheet and covered Kulu's cage. I swear, for a moment, a look of relief crossed her tiny beaked face. With everything that had happened tonight, I was amazed that she hadn't died of a heart attack.

"Goodnight, Kulu," I whispered.

I was halfway to my bedroom, when a tiny voice squawked, "Goodnight, Harry."

At 7 a.m. a chorus of barks, growls, screeches and shrieks awakened me. Jimmy and the crew from Splatz had arrived. He strolled through my kitchen and living room, checking boxes on his clipboard, raising his brows and uttering an occasional grunt. Between sips of my first cup of coffee, I worked up the guts to ask him what this mess was going to cost me.

He laughed like a hyena. "More than you make in a year."

I reminded him how much business I send his way, so he agreed that we'd be square if I'd write him a five-star review on Yelp and appear in a Splatz TV commercial. Done and done. He had me over the proverbial barrel. What choice did I have?

I looked at my watch. I had to meet Cap at twelve. "Can you be finished by eleven-thirty?"

"You're shitting me." Jimmy sighed and ran his hands through his hair. "Even with industrial fans and separate crews for cleaning, carpentry and painting, we're talking two p.m. Earliest."

A quiet rap on my back door interrupted the conversation. Mrs. Nussbaum stood on my porch, peeking through the curtains.

I opened the door but blocked her line of sight by standing on the threshold.

"Who dose mens?" she asked, craning her neck to see past me and into the house.

"Plumbers."

She stooped and shoved her head below my outstretched arm. "Why big plastic sheet hanging—"

"There's shit and pee everywhere, Mrs. N. Gotta run, now. Bye-bye." I slammed the door and exhaled slowly. That was close. Then it occurred to me that even though I could put Headbutt outside while the crew worked, Kulu wouldn't be able to handle the fumes from the cleaning solutions.

I threw open the door and yelled, "Mrs. Nussbaum? Could I

leave my bird at your house today? Just for a couple of hours? The fumes could hurt her lungs."

Mrs. Nussbaum frowned. "Why my house? Mens just fixing toilet."

"All that shit and pee? And those nasty chemicals? Burn her feathers right off."

"Bah!" Nosy Nonnie snarled. "Fine. I take bird. But if it bite, I cook it."

I grabbed Kulu's cage, reinforced the no biting rule, and raced outside. "Thanks. I owe you one, Mrs. Nussbaum."

Before she could reply, I was halfway back to the porch. *No take backs*, I thought, as I dove through the door, slamming it closed behind me.

Jimmy chuckled. "So, now we're plumbers?"

"Damn straight. That's my story, and I'm sticking to it."

I showered and dressed for my meeting with Cap. Then, I put Headbutt outside before I left, scolding him, and begging him to cut Mrs. N. some slack today. If not for her sake, then for mine. I don't think he gave a rat's ass. He loved to push her buttons. We have a lot in common, Headbutt and I.

On my way out the door, I hesitated before tucking Veronica's book back inside my duster. It was evidence that needed to be turned over. So why was I wavering?

As I drove to the 51st, it occurred to me that I hadn't been there since Harry's death. That had only been a day and a half ago. But it seemed like a lifetime. Cap's watchdog, Miriam, manned her post as usual but with an uncharacteristic lack of zeal. Her eyes were bloodshot, like she'd been crying.

"I'm sorry about Harry, Ms. Nighthawk. I know you were close. Such a good man."

Another awkward condolence. After a quick nod, I glanced at Cap's door. "We have a noon meeting."

Miriam buzzed Cap and then ushered me into his office. She flashed a faint smile, as if rewarding me for my compliance with her rules. Totally unintended on my part. I wasn't in the mood to play.

When Miriam closed the door behind her, Cap stood, motioning toward his guest chairs. "Have a seat, please." His eyes swept to my bandaged hand. "How you doing?"

"Ready, willing and able."

His gaze remained fixed on my hand. Apparently, the ride in had reopened my cuts. Fresh blood seeped out from beneath the Band-Aids. "What happened there?"

"It's nothing. I just broke a glass."

Cap nodded. "Harry's brother, Ralph, is on his way into town. He'll be making Harry's arrangements." Cap looked away and cleared his throat. "He hemmed and hawed about the bird, but eventually agreed to take it. I'll have a squad car drive him to your house this afternoon to pick it up."

Screw Ralph.

Cap perched on the corner of his desk. "I wanted to thank you for your help on the Henry case. Harry told me how much he enjoyed working with you. But now that you've raised Ms. Henry and exhausted the paranormal aspect of the investigation, your work is finished."

"Excuse me?"

"You did what Harry needed you to do. You raised Veronica and extracted what little information she could provide. End of story—"

"But—"

"I know you helped Harry investigate beyond that. And yes, I allowed it. But that's not what you're contracted to do. Harry's dead. His murder could be connected to this case. You could get hurt, or worse. I'm sorry, but I won't accept the responsibility of your further involvement. You're off the case."

"My involvement produced information we would never had gotten otherwise. Harry was murdered because we were getting too close to the truth. Don't cut me out now."

"You're not to touch the Henry case, or Harry's murder. Have I made myself clear?"

"Crystal."

"You're still on retainer for paranormal investigations. I'll be in touch."

So many thoughts and emotions surged through me at once. Even the brain bitch was speechless.

Cap stood up and walked me to the door. "The DA's office called this morning, requesting Harry's file on the Henry murder. You two never found the book Ms. Henry mentioned, did you?"

Harry's warning played in my head. Trusting the wrong person could get me killed.

"No, sir," I said, without batting an eye. "We never did."

I left Cap's office with Veronica's leather book still tucked inside my duster.

Little Allie fumed. *"You should have given it to him."*

I'd have laid odds that Cap's name wasn't in those pages, but that's where my certainty stopped. There were too many powerful people with too much to lose. They'd stop at nothing to destroy that book, if they knew of its existence.

And at least one of them knew. At least one of them had me in their sights, drugging my dog, leaving me dead flounders and flowers, and even orchestrating my own personal biter attack. (Rather insulting, actually, to think I couldn't handle a single corpsicle.) And then there was Harry. Dead Harry, who'd apparently solved the case and was murdered before he could prove it.

Like hell I'm off the case, I thought. I slammed through the doors of the 51st and into the midday sun.

Fuck 'em all, Harry. I'm going to finish what we started.

———

The meeting with Cap had been short and sweet. Jimmy and the Splatz crew needed more time with my house, so I decided to stop into The Blue Note for lunch. Dallas eyed the bloody Band-Aids on my hand.

"How 'bout a burger and fries?" I said, settling onto a bar stool.

"Let's have a look at that hand." He pulled the first aid kit out from beneath the bar. Slipping on his glasses, he inspected my hand by the light of the old banker's lamp next to the cash register.

"You'll live," he said, dressing the wounds and rewrapping my entire hand. "Keep it clean and dry. And for God's sake, let the damn thing heal."

He walked to the sink and washed his hands.

"What time do you want me tonight?"

"Did you hear what I said?"

"I need money."

"You can't wash glasses, carry food or pour drinks. What are you going to do?"

"I'll work one-handed."

"How you going to get back and forth?"

"Uber." *Big fat liar.*

He shook his head and tossed my burger on the grill. "Suit yourself. Stubborn ass."

I let that slide. He fixes a mean burger. And I was starved. Besides, he was right.

I tooled back into my driveway at 2 p.m. on the nose, anxious to see the house. Jimmy and his gang were packing up their gear. He walked me through the interior, letting me inspect their work. Good as new. Even better. They saved me the trouble of repainting the living room that hadn't been painted in twenty years, give or take.

I followed him out to his truck and thanked him for finishing the job so quickly.

"No problem, Nighthawk." He reached into his glovebox and handed me an official Splatz air freshener for the car I didn't own. "Only my A-list clients get one of these. I'll be in touch about those TV spots."

As the Splatz crew backed out of the driveway, a squad car pulled up along the curb. A guy who looked a lot like Harry heaved himself out of the back seat. Ralph Delk had come for Kulu. It made sense, giving him the bird. I needed another pet like I needed a hole in the head. Ralph even walked like Harry as he trudged across the yard.

"You must be Nighthawk," he said, extending his hand. "I'm Harry's brother, Ralph. I understand he had some sort of bird."

After offering my condolences for the loss of his brother, I asked him to hang loose a minute while I ran next door to rescue Kulu from Mrs. Nussbaum.

She opened the door before I even reached her porch and thrust Kulu's cage at me. "Take. Is nasty, nasty bird."

"Crazy bitch! Crazy bitch!" Kulu screeched, and ricocheted off the bars of her cage like a feathered pinball.

Nonnie sneered. "*Bah! Meshuge farshtunken foygl.* Crazy, stinky bird! No bring back," she said, slamming her door in my face.

I carried Kulu across the lawn, wondering how that scene had played to Ralph.

"Don't mind my neighbor," I said, handing him the cage. "She's not much of an animal lover."

"Me neither." He frowned at Kulu through the bars like she was an alien life form. "But that's not your problem. Right, Ms. Nighthawk? C'mon, bird," he said, plodding back toward the cruiser.

"Wait. Don't you want her food or Harry's bird book?"

"Whatever." He shrugged and glared at Kulu. "Maybe I'll set you free, huh? Let you fly away so you can play with the other birds."

In the dead of winter?

I jogged to the curb and wrenched the cage from his hand.

"Ralph, Kulu's a tropical bird. Why don't I just hang onto her?" I started back to the house and called over my shoulder, "Thanks for stopping by. See you at the service."

"Suit yourself," he mumbled, trundling himself back into the cruiser.

I lifted Kulu's cage and peered through its bars. "No offense, bird, but your Uncle Ralph's a real asshat."

"Ralph's an asshat," she said, shaking her flaming-red tail feathers. "Big ol' asshat."

As God is my witness, I heard Harry laugh. And just like that, I knew I'd made the right decision. Kulu was home to stay.

21

JESUS WEPT

Less than three hours later, I showed up for my shift at The Blue Note. Dallas, focused on my hand, wanted to plant me at the cash register, i.e., a night with no tips. After a profanity-laced argument, he agreed that I could serve customers if I wore a nitrile glove over my bandages. A wasted squabble, really. The typical Saturday night crowd, mostly Coke-suckers and darters, were notoriously bad tippers. I was hoping Tiffany would drop in. One of us needed to apologize to the other. I had a feeling it was me. But the night wore on with no sign of the six-foot drama queen, and I didn't give her further thought until a call came in around ten o'clock.

"For you," Dallas said, as I bustled out of the kitchen with an order of wings.

He handed me the phone, I handed him my tray and wondered who the hell would call me there.

"Miss Allie Nighthawk?"

"Yes?"

"This is Nurse Decker calling from the emergency department of Christ Hospital. A patient named Tiffany Swarovski asked that we contact you at this number. Your presence is urgently requested."

My stomach lurched. "Is... Is she okay?"

"The doctor will provide more details when you arrive."

I slumped onto a barstool. "Is she...alive?"

A somber-looking Dallas waited at my elbow, still holding the tray of wings.

"Yes, she is alive. But we do ask that you arrive as quickly and safely as possible."

"Of course," I said, disconnecting the call.

Dallas steadied himself at the bar. "What's the matter?"

"It's Tiffany. She's in the ER at Christ Hospital, and she's asking for me." I grabbed my gear, hurtled out from behind the bar and broke for the door.

Dallas called after me. "Is she sick? Hurt...or what?"

"I'll let you know."

The streets were deserted at that hour of the night. I could make the normally fifteen-minute drive to Clifton in ten if I went full throttle. Once I hit fifth gear, I stayed there. *She's alive,* I told myself as the bitter wind buffeted my face. *If she were dead, she couldn't have asked them to call you.*

I flew up Auburn Hill and into the parking garage, then followed the signs to the ER. Even late at night, the waiting room was packed. I marched inside, past the registration clerk, and through the double doors to the treatment area.

A weathered-looking nurse sat by the window, reading a chart. "May I help you?" she asked, peering over a pair of half-moon cheaters.

"I'm here for Tiffany Swarovski."

"Are you her next of kin?"

"Ah…sure."

The nurse frowned. "Only next of kin—"

"You called me, lady. Check it out. Nighthawk. Allie Nighthawk. Take me to her or I'll—"

"The doctor is with Ms. Sworovski now. We'll call you back when he's ready to meet with you. And keep your voice down, please. This is a hospital."

I shot her the Allie eye, but lowered my voice. "What happened to Tiffany?"

"The doctor will fill you in when he sees you."

I leaned against the corner of the nurse's station and stared down the hallway, scrutinizing the treatment bays, hoping to pick up Tiffany's vibe. Two of Cincinnati's finest milled around the last treatment bay in the row. The officers whispered among themselves and paced, arms folded, as if they were waiting to see whoever was inside. Feet shuffled back and forth behind the drawn privacy curtain.

Vibes or no vibes, the odds were in my favor that I'd found Tiffany.

I slipped around the corner of the nurse's station and made a beeline to the furthest treatment bay.

"Evening, officers," I said, pointing to the curtain. "Is Tiffany Sworovski in there?"

The older of the two officers cocked his eye. "And you would be?"

"Allie Nighthawk. I worked with Harry Delk, out of the 51st. Maybe you knew him?"

The cop's eyes flashed with instant recognition, followed by sorrow. "I sure did. Good man, Harry. Sorry for your loss." He cleared his throat and nodded at the curtain. "Yeah. That's Ms. Swarovski."

"What happened to her?"

"She was stabbed and left for dead. Somebody called an ambulance an hour — maybe an hour and a half ago."

"Did she see who attacked her?"

"She saw the guy, but didn't recognize him."

"How bad is she?"

The curtain opened and the ER doc stepped out.

"Officers and..." he referred to his chart, "Ms. Nighthawk, I presume?"

"Yes. That's me."

"Ms. Swarovski is in critical condition. She sustained sharp force trauma to her neck and chest, resulting in significant blood loss and shock. A CT and angiography of her neck revealed a right vertebral artery injury. She's headed into surgery."

Oh, God. No, no, no. "Will she... Is she...going to make it?"

He flashed a weary smile. "She's in good hands. That's the best I can say. Let the surgeons work their magic. She's sedated now, but she asked for you. She told me to tell you, and I quote, 'They're after the book.' Whatever that means. You can sit with her if you like, until the orderly arrives." He turned to the officers. "Any other questions?"

"No, thanks. We got what we need," the old cop answered.

As the doctor walked away, the cop darted his eyes to me. "What's this book she was talking about?"

Crap. Crap. Crap. "Sorry, guys. I wish I could say. After Harry's death, Captain Dorsey took me off the case. I only showed up because Tiffany asked for me. Now, if you don't mind..." I ducked behind the curtain for a private moment with Tiffany, hoping the officers would consider their investigation temporarily concluded until Tiffany made it out of surgery.

Little Allie stuck me like a pin. *IF she makes it out of surgery.*

Within seconds, the officers wandered away, leaving me to sit with Tiffany in peace. I'm not great with words. What I had to say wouldn't take long.

I held her hand. It was cold as a corpse.

I leaned down to her ear and whispered, "Thank you, sista. I owe you. Just make sure you're around to collect."

The curtain swung back, and the orderly wheeled a gurney beside Tiffany's bed.

I squeezed her hand one last time and murmured, "Later, chica."

Nurse Ratched glared at me from the nurse's station as I hustled to catch the elevator. I threw her a condescending wink, but didn't stop to chat. I was on a mission. If I didn't solve this case soon, that book of Veronica's, written in freaking Klingon, would be the death of everyone involved.

Something nagged me as I headed home, up 71 North. Despite Harry's warning about our shrinking circle of trust, should I have told Cap about the book? It was the one piece of evidence I'd kept to myself. Turning it over could bring us closer to the killer. But if the names of prominent city officials appeared in those pages, they'd stop at nothing to keep the contents of that book from reaching the light of day.

I decided, once again, to sit on it. For now. I wanted one more shot at deciphering the code. Failing that, I'd have no choice but to throw caution to the wind and turn the book over to someone who could. But who's to say it wouldn't disappear?

I coasted into my driveway around one thirty in the morning and slipped into my house, certain that I'd made the right decision. While Headbutt took a quick pee break (on or off Mrs. Nussbaum's rose bushes for all I cared), I covered Kulu for the night and fixed a Jack Daniel's slushie.

After slipping into Harry's *Ballistic Therapy* T-shirt, I let Headbutt back in. We curled up on my freshly slipcovered couch to read Veronica's little black book, with its pristine cover and tiny lettering. An icy, warming sip from my slushie trickled down my throat. *Relax*, I told myself. *Focus. Let your eyes absorb what you're reading.*

I followed my own advice. Twenty pages in, I still had shit. The damn thing was a six by four, eighty-page cryptogram.

"How hard can this be, Harry?" I whispered. "Help me out, here."

I closed my eyes and swirled a mouthful of Jack between my cheeks, picturing a calm, serene ocean gleaming in the moonlight. Determined to break the code, I tried again. The net result: Jack shit.

"Damn it," I screamed, flinging the book across the room and into the kitchen. All I needed was one stinking break. Veronica Henry was dead. Harry was dead. And for all I knew, Tiffany could be dead by now. Everyone connected to this piece of shit book was dead, except me. And there I sat, with my thumb up my ass. The only other evidence, Veronica's phone and financial records, were MIA, possibly destroyed. Recreating them would take time — time I didn't have. It was up to me to solve the case, but I had no fucking clue how. And no one left to help me.

I curled into a ball and pulled my knees to my chest.

Harry's voice whirred in my ear. "Jesus wept, Nighthawk. Look at the freaking book."

I sprang to my feet, almost afraid I'd find Harry beside me. But it was only Headbutt, staring at me like I'd lost my mind.

"Sleep," I mumbled, rubbing my eyes. "A good night's sleep then I'll go back to the book tomorrow, one last time."

I padded into the kitchen to pick up the book and found its soft leather cover wedged inside the kickplate grille of the refrigerator. After several tugs, I freed the book, only to find the end sheet, glued to the inside cover, had ripped and was partially peeled back.

I smoothed the end sheet down against the cover, and a faint outline rose beneath my fingertips. Something thin and very small was tucked between the cover and the end sheet. After several attempts to tease it out with my fingers, I grabbed one of my gunsmith screwdrivers, slid it along the outline, and freed a folded piece of paper that could break this case wide open.

"Thanks for the assist, Harry," I whispered, staring at a neatly printed web address: www.rainydaybacon.com.

22

NOT EXACTLY BATTING A THOUSAND

To hell with a good night's sleep. I fired up my laptop and typed in the web address. My fingers moved at the speed of light, tripping over the keys several times before entering the right digits in the right sequence. Not that it made much difference. The site was password protected.

I tried a couple of combinations that seemed obvious: Veronica Hoi, Stretchoi, and her parents' and siblings' names. Of course, they didn't work. Veronica was a smart cookie. Unlocking her password wouldn't be easy. She would have made sure of that. But one way or another, I'd get into that site. Irritation aside, the book might be the quickest route to the information I needed. So, I put on a pot of coffee and settled in for an all-nighter.

How long could it take to crack the code?

The handwritten scrawl resembled hieroglyphics. After a couple of passes at the text, I realized the book contained both characters and symbols. Periodically, symbols separated one or two characters, like dashes between months, days and years. Sometimes, symbols appeared after a string of three or four characters, followed by two more characters. Dollar amounts? It was a reasonable hypothesis. But nothing more.

Next came the tedious part: substitution by trial and error. I searched for one letter words. I's and A's. Then three letter words. The T's, H's, and E's leapt off the page. I guzzled more coffee and started over. Lather, rinse, repeat, again and again — each pass followed by more coffee.

By the time the S's revealed themselves, the pot was dry and the sun was up. I hadn't decoded much, but enough to see that the book contained names, dates, notes and dollar amounts. My eyes were crossing. I needed a break. Little Allie bombarded my brain with visions of Tiffany, lying in the hospital, suffering, or worse. She should be out of surgery by now, I thought. The book could wait another hour or two. After letting Headbutt out to do his business, I fed him and Kulu, shoved the book inside my duster for safekeeping, then jumped on my Harley and headed back to Christ Hospital.

After a quick stop by patient information for Tiffany's room number, I rode the elevator to the third floor, then wound through the maze of hallways in search of room 327.

Her door was partially closed. I listened from the hallway, making sure I wouldn't be interrupting something that neither one of us would have wanted me to see. The coast was clear. As I slipped into her room, the quiet beep-beep of monitors that tracked her heart beat and respirations pinged in my ears. The cushion on the visitor's recliner farted when I sat down.

Tiffany opened one eye and frowned. "Where the hell you been?"

"They took you to surgery, so I went home."

She snorted and turned away.

"*Geez.* I came back."

"Too little, too late." She shifted in her bed and grimaced. "I be mad at you later. They know you got the book."

Given everything that had transpired, I'd already reached that conclusion. But I wasn't above yanking her chain. "You squealed?"

"Not right away. After the second stab wound, I figured they was serious. Gave you up like a bad habit."

"Well, no harm, no foul." I stared out the window, rather than meet her gaze. "I put you in the middle of all this. Sorry."

"Damn straight, you did. You owe me, too. Got a spare lung?"

My heart skipped a beat, and the room began to spin. I figured I'd already owe Nonnie a kidney someday, since she wouldn't accept dog biscuits in lieu of cash. Now Tiffany needed a lung? I was losing body parts faster than green grass shoots through a goose.

Tiffany laughed, then winced and grabbed her chest. "Shit, that hurt. But it was worth it. I don't need no lung. Shoulda seen your face."

"Bite me."

"Kinky shit cost you a pinky finger."

I snickered and changed the subject. "There was a web address hidden in Veronica's book, www.rainydaybacon.com. Know anything about it?"

Tiffany pressed the button on her pain pump and shook her head. "Can't say I do."

"You wouldn't know any of Veronica's passwords?"

"Sure. All us hoes use the same passwords." She halfheartedly reached through the bed rail and tried to smack me. "No, I don't know her fucking passwords!"

"You were closer to her than anyone else on the street. What was the name of her first pet?"

"How would I know that? We wasn't born joined at the hip, dumbass!"

There was a chance she'd know some obscure information, so my irritating questions continued. Did she know where Veronica went to grade school? The name of her childhood best friend? Her mother's maiden name? What street she grew up on? Yadda-yadda-yadda.

"She have a lucky number?" I asked.

After a pause, Tiffany blurted, "Thirteen. Said nobody else liked it 'cause it was unlucky. And her mama was born on the thirteenth."

"Her favorite drink?"

"Whatever the guy was buying."

"She have a favorite lotto pick?"

"I only saw her buy one lotto ticket in my life." Tiffany's eyes grew wide. "She played her mama's birthday—"

"Which was?"

"What the... How the hell should I know? Something thirteen, nineteen something, something. I gotta do everything for you? Go on now, leave me be. You're harshin' my buzz."

I stood and walked to the door, then stopped and turned around. "I'll find whoever did this to you. I promise."

"Good luck with that, baby," Tiffany said, closing her eyes. "You ain't exactly batting a thousand."

Everyone's a critic. I had some huge shoes to fill with Harry gone. Who killed Veronica? Who killed Harry? Who attacked Tiffany? I hoped that when I found my bogie, the answers to my questions wouldn't be far behind.

Screw Nonnie Nussbaum. I tore up Pitty Pat Lane and ramped the curb at the end of my driveway, then skidded to a stop and burst through the door, into my house.

Headbutt launched six inches into the air from his spot on the vent and crashed back to the floor.

Kulu fluttered furiously, screeching, "What the fuck?"

I was on a mission.

I opened my laptop, flopped onto the couch and pulled up www.rainydaybacon.com, determined to find the password. Veronica's name, her initials, her age, her date of birth combined with countless numerical sequences. Nope. Tiffany's name, her nickname, Stretch. Veronica's mother's name, her father's, brother's, both sisters' and her cousins' names with those same numerical sequences and more. Wrong again.

This was hopeless. Like finding a needle in a haystack. *Think. Think. What information did I know about Veronica, and where had I learned it?* Veronica was twenty-three years old. That was in the case file at the ME's office. Her BFF was Tiffany, aka Stretch. According to Tiffany, Veronica's mother's date of birth was her favorite lottery pick. The 13th of (name that month), during 19 (pick a year).

The conversations Harry and I had with Veronica's family members looped through my brain, but nothing meaningful stood out, except something her mother had said. She'd given birth to Veronica when she was eighteen. Twenty-three plus eighteen made Veronica's mother forty-one years old. So, she was born in, using my fingers, borrowing the one, and grimacing to wake up long forgotten brain cells…1977. Ah ha! Her birthday was something 13, 1977.

Was I on the right track? I'd know soon enough.

I typed in Veronica01131977, then Veronica02131977, and finished the sequence. Still no dice. Then I entered Stretch with the same numerical sequence. When I typed in Stretch06131977 the site opened wide.

A list of dated and time stamped videos popped up. I opened the first video and almost peed myself. Veronica had filmed her sessions with her clients! The videos weren't poorly lit, grainy footage of their private parts either. Their faces were clear as a bell. And some of them, surprisingly familiar.

Damn. Was there anyone she hadn't been doing?

I cross-checked the video dates against the partially decoded dates in the book, then matched faces with half-deciphered names and amounts, which helped me fill in the missing letters. The pieces came together. The videos were posted in date order, first to last, matching the entries in the book. Veronica had her ducks in a nice, neat little row.

I opened the video from the date of her murder and nearly fell out of my chair when the killer's face came into view. Son of a bitch! I knew that bastard. A quick cross-check against Veronica's book found that he was into her for twenty grand! Why didn't that surprise me?

The motion-activated camera in her bedroom filmed our guy taking her from behind, placing one hand beneath her chin and stabbing her in the back, military style. Just like the ME report stated. She'd never seen it coming. The entire episode, from start to finish, caught on film. Holy guacamole!

I pulled out my phone and dialed Cap's number. Miriam answered. I was so excited, I didn't even bother to abuse her. She put me through and he picked up on the first ring.

"Whatever it is, I don't want to hear it," he barked. "You're off the case, remember?"

"I know who killed Veronica Henry! I can't explain on the phone. Just come to my house, *now*. And for God's sake, don't tell a soul where you're going."

23

GAME ON, BABY!

I sprang from the couch, high-fived the air, and hit the coffee pot for a congratulatory refill. It was still empty from my all-night marathon session, so I made a new batch. Headbutt woofed, hauling his considerable butt off the floor vent and did his pee-pee dance. After a stern but futile warning to avoid Nonnie's rose bushes, I let him out, closed the door, and watched the tubby troublemaker through the kitchen window. He and I understood each other. But I didn't trust that chonker as far as I could throw him.

My thoughts drifted to Harry. About how proud he'd be that I cracked the case on my own. Oh, he'd bust my chops about how it took a village and a roadmap to help me. But that was just our way. He'd know I'd never rest until I saw it through. He'd buy me a Jack Daniel's, then I'd slide him a boilermaker on the house, and we'd be cool. If only I could see him...

A knock at the front door pulled me out of the deep, dark hole I was about to step into. Kulu screeched a sassy, "Get the hell outta here," as I crossed the living room and opened the door to let Cap in.

Only it wasn't Cap.

"Good morning, Ms. Nighthawk. Sorry for the interruption. I'd like a minute of your time." DA Farragut hovered inside the glass screen door, just past the threshold. His eyes, intense and overly bright, swept past me, into the house.

"Now?" I asked, planting my feet. "It's not a good time. I'll swing by your office later."

I held the interior door, blocking his entrance, but he pushed past me.

"This will only take a minute."

Kulu flapped and fluttered in her cage, then broke into a chorus of "Bad Boys."

Farragut chuckled. "Smart bird."

"Smarter than you know," I said, backing away from the door and casually putting the couch between us. "How can I help you?"

"You're withholding evidence in the Henry case. Hand it over. Now."

He stepped forward, but I held my ground, feigning a smile. "What evidence?"

"Don't play games. Veronica Henry's book."

"What book?"

"The book she told you about when you raised her."

"Oh, that book. Don't you want the video, too?"

Suddenly the cat had his tongue, and I couldn't help but rub his nose in it. "Oh, there's a ton of videos. But I'm guessing the one you'd want is the video of you murdering Veronica."

His eyes blazed. "There's no vid—"

"Actually, there is," I said, "but I'll be hanging onto it. And the book, too."

He pulled a Glock 19 and nudged the couch sideways with his leg. "If you think I'm going down for killing that whore, think again."

"Is that the gun you used to kill Harry?"

"Who says I did?"

He nudged the couch again.

"Oh, please," I said, moving in tandem. "He had you dead to rights when you killed him. How'd you break in without him hearing you? Or did you knock on his door, too?"

"Here I am, with my gun aimed right between your eyes, and you're wondering how I killed Harry."

Farragut had a point. My weapons were holstered and hanging from a chair in my bedroom. Headbutt, my zombie-hunting rescue dog, was outside, whizzing on everybody's bushes but mine. I seemed to be at a disadvantage

Click.

Nothing like the metallic click of a safety to sharpen your focus.

Farragut raised his arm. I hurled a couch pillow at him, and he flinched. The 9mm slug from his Glock drilled a hole in my ceiling.

"I just had that repainted, damn it!"

Game on, baby!

I launched myself across the couch at Farragut and grabbed his gun hand.

A second shot rang out.

The bullet slammed into the bars of the wrought iron bird cage and toppled it to the floor. Its door popped open. A frantic Kulu spiraled out into the room.

Farragut and I crashed to the floor together, neither willing to let go of the gun. Over and over we rolled, kicking and thrashing, each of us trying to gain the upper hand. He cranked my wrist and wrenched the gun away from me, but I kneed him in his nards. A low groan filled my ears as he doubled over. I rolled onto my side and snap-kicked the gun from his hand. When his eyes followed the Glock, I reared back and slammed that same foot into his jaw. He rolled over twice and landed face down. I scrambled to my feet, gasping for air, never taking my eyes from him. He was out like a light. But for how long?

Farragut was a big dude. And he was bound to wake up miffed. I needed to confiscate his gun. It lay in front of him, out of his reach. He still hadn't moved. His breathing was rhythmic and steady. There'd be no better time.

I stepped across Farragut, bent down and reached for the Glock.

He punched the back of my knee, bringing me down.

I lunged for the gun, but he flipped me over onto my back. A seven-inch Ka-Bar knife, just like mine, flanked my jaw.

Damn, Cap. Where the hell are you?

Farragut pushed the tip of the knife into my neck and drew a bead of blood. "I've been wanting to do this since the day we met."

The storm door exploded into a thousand shards of glass as Headbutt sailed into the house like an eighty-pound, sausage-shaped cannon ball. He clamped onto Farragut's knife hand and shook him like a rag doll. Kulu went into Pterodactyl mode and tag teamed for an assist, swooping in and pecking at the DA's face and eyes.

Farragut screamed.

A car door slammed outside. Seconds later, Cap burst through the shattered storm door, gun drawn. His eyes dove straight to Kulu and Headbutt, gnawing on Cincinnati's District Attorney.

"Don't shoot my dog! Or my bird!" I screamed. "Headbutt, *stop.*"

For the first time in his life, Headbutt obeyed me. He let go of Farragut's arm, trotted to my side and lay down. Kulu fluttered away and perched on the living room curtain rod.

Cap eyed me, then Farragut, then me again. "What the hell's going on?"

"Our friendly DA here murdered Veronica Henry."

"That's an outright lie," Farragut shouted. "I had no reason to kill that woman."

My jaw dropped. "You were into her for twenty grand. She had you by the balls. I'd call that plenty of motive."

"You lying little—"

"And then you killed Harry, you son of a bitch."

"You're delusional," Farragut said, climbing to his feet. He darted his eyes to Cap. "I'd be very careful with your next move, Captain. Your career is at stake."

"Don't let him go. I've got proof!" I said, racing to my computer.

Cap grudgingly held his gun on Farragut while I played the video and turned over Veronica's book. Nighthawk: One. Farragut: Zero. The DA was going down for the count.

After the video ended, while Cap was slapping his cuffs on the city's district attorney, I set Kulu's cage upright.

"Harry's killer," the mouthy feather duster shrieked. "Harry's killer!"

I was about to ask Cap if Kulu could testify in court, when Nonnie Nussbaum charged through my kitchen door. "Mrs. Nighthawk! Headbutt dig hole under fence. Is running loose. Naughty, naughty golem!"

So, that's how my favorite chonk of a zombie hunter got loose and crashed through the storm door. (For those counting, that was the second time he'd saved my ass.) As I escorted Nonnie back outside, her eyes darted into the living room, scanning the sea of broken glass and two strange men she'd never seen before.

"Who dose mens?"

"Plumbers."

"Again, with the plumbers? And why the glass—"

"Bye, bye, Nonnie," I said, closing the door with a sigh.

Someday, heaven forbid, I might have to tell her what I really do for a living.

24

I'M JUST WILD ABOUT HARRY

The following weekend, Dallas held a wake for Harry Delk, complete with bar food, half-priced drinks, and a framed picture of the old dinosaur, hunched in his favorite stool at the end of the bar. Harry would have approved. Even if I did have a hard time drinking to his memory.

Harry's brother, Ralph, had already left town, so the gathering was small. Jimmy McQueen and Hank Bowers popped in. Tiffany, who'd only been out the hospital for a couple of days, stopped by, wearing a gold lamé mini-dress and purple stilettos. She wanted to toast Harry, plus she had some exciting news to share.

"I'm done with the streets. Too much drama-rama, baby. Got me an agent, now — says I'm wrestlicious."

I cocked an eyebrow.

"Wrestlicious. Lady wrestling, girl." She clawed the air with her flaming red nails. "He's gonna pimp me out to the WWE. Travel the world, make me some big bucks."

Who was I to judge? Wrestling might be the perfect fit for her, not to mention legal. She had a good six inches and seventy-pounds on me. Her metallic bustier and fishnet hose would look normal for a change. And she could trash talk with the best. I should know.

Opie showed up to pay his respects too, with Cap dragging in, not far behind. Opie had some interesting gossip of his own.

"Word on the street is Mark Andrews will take over for Farragut."

"The senior ADA." Cap whistled. "Nighthawk, the two of you are going to be like oil and water."

"No surprise, there. Haven't met a DA yet I can get along with."

Opie snorted. "Is there anyone you do get along with?"

I thought about that question and then raised my Jack Daniel's high. "To Harry Delk. The best partner I ever had, that I never wanted in the first place. He was funny, smart, and a damn fine zombie hunter. I liked Harry. I...I got along with Harry."

"To Harry," came the universal reply.

We clinked glasses, and I turned to swipe my eyes. Tough as nails Harry wouldn't have appreciated tears.

"I've been thinking," Opie said, "with Farragut going away, and Andrews likely taking over, there'll be some openings in the DA's office. I might apply."

"Doesn't the defense side pay better?" I asked.

"You were my first case in months, courtesy of Harry. And you didn't pay squat. To Harry," Opie said, raising his glass.

I joined Opie's toast for Harry's sake, but that toast was just plain mean.

"Now that you're all together," Dallas said, "I have an announcement. I got a brother down in Florida. He and his twenty-seven-footer's been calling my name for years. I'm closing up shop here, for now. But I'm not going to sell the place. I want to keep my options open. Sorry, Allie Cat. Looks like you're out of a job, for now. You're a damn fine bartender. Be happy to give you a good reference."

Perfect. I'd come back into town with two packs of Ramen Noodles in my pocket. Since then, I'd accumulated a sausage-shaped cannonball and a foul-mouthed feather duster to feed. I was cash poor and 'animals with attitudes' rich.

Like I said before, zombie hunting isn't everything it's cracked up to be.

About nine o'clock, Cap checked his watch and slid off his bar stool. He laid his money on the bar and headed to the door.

"Where you think you're going?" I asked.

"Got a date," he said with a wink.

That got my vote for the most surprising news of the night.

After Jimmy, Hank, and most of the other regulars had paid their tabs and gone home, Dallas strolled to the juke box and slipped in a quarter. Peggy Lee started crooning, "I'm Just Wild About Harry."

Now that. That was the classiest tribute of the night.

Dallas, Opie, Tiffany and I lost ourselves in Harry stories, and before I knew it, midnight had arrived. The phone rang, catching us all by surprise.

Dallas answered, then handed the call to me with a whisper, "It's the precinct."

Shit shit shitty-shit shit. "Ah...huh. Ah huh." I held the phone away from my ear while I listened. "Yes. But I'm freaking always on call. I've been at a wake for Harry Delk all night. Can't one of the uniforms take it?"

Cap's second in command, Lieutenant Benson, wasn't taking no for an answer.

I hopped off my stool. "Where'd you say this was? Yeah. Okay. Be there as soon as I can."

I walked into Dallas's office to get my coat and weapons. I sheathed my knife, and slipped into my holster. When I came back out and rounded the bar, Dallas looked disappointed.

"Sorry. Gotta go," I said, throwing on my duster. "There's a biter call at Spring Grove Cemetery."

25

LIFE AMONG THE TOMBSTONES

Rain sprinkled my face as I walked out of The Blue Note. A storm was rolling in from the west — exactly where I was headed. I pulled on my rain gear, watched lightning split the night sky, then counted Mississippi's and waited for thunder. *Good*, I thought, tilting my face to the sky, and letting the cold drops energize me. The storm was still miles off. With any luck, I'd reach the cemetery before that lightning found me and my bike.

I pulled out of the parking lot with my eyes glued to the road. Once I reached cruising speed, I eased back on the throttle and relaxed. There are two things that can get a person killed on a bike: overconfidence and fear. I had way too much to do to wake up dead.

Sprinkles turned into showers. The brain bitch hounded me as I drove down I-75. *Something's wrong.* No shit, Sherlock. The last time I'd taken a late night biter call in an obscure place it turned out to be a set up. Harry and I had to hold off a freaking horde before CPD showed up to help us out.

Harry isn't here to hold your hand this time, the head hag wheedled.

The whiny little bitch could pound salt. This run wouldn't be any different than a thousand other calls I'd successfully handled on my own. Self-doubt was another thing that could get me killed. Perfect time to second guess me, you loud-mouthed earwig.

The wind began to gust as I pulled up to the main gate of Spring Grove Cemetery, where the security guard paced back and forth, waiting for me. Benny, as he introduced himself, had already unlocked and opened the gate.

"The security cameras picked up the rotter in section twenty," he said, pointing into the distance. "Straight ahead, then to the left. Just north of Geyser Lake."

My gut instantly soured, and I wondered why. It's not like this was my first rodeo. Stormy, late night cemetery runs are what you'd call my wheelhouse.

Little Allie scoffed. *You know perfectly well why.*

I booted her and her snarky bullshit into a dusty corner of my mind, and threatened to lock them away forever. When I turned to ask Benny if he could stick around in case things went sideways, he was halfway back to his security shack. The freaking weasel.

I climbed off the Lowrider, switched on my flashlight and trudged through the darkness.

The serene, well-tended grounds looked different at night. Almost...alive. The earth rose and fell, twisted and turned, like a tilt-a-whirl in a funhouse. Rain showers morphed into downpours. Drops pelted my eyes and ricocheted off tree limbs. Lightning snaked across the sky followed by an instantaneous, earthshaking boom. Shapeless shadows darted through the trees. Whispers whirred around me.

My neck prickled and I jumped at the snap of my own footfalls.

Why? Why was I so afraid?

The brain bitch's words haunted me. *You know perfectly well why.*

"Enough," I shouted into the storm. "Enough already."

For crap's sake. I'd lived my entire life among the tombstones. I'd raised and put down the dead in the shadow of monuments and markers since I was eleven years old. I am my mother's daughter — a corpse whisperer. And there wasn't one damn thing different about tonight than any other night.

So why did my stomach ache with dread?

You know why.

That thought hadn't sprung from inside me. And it hadn't come from Little Allie, either.

Open your eyes, an intruder whispered in my mind. *See the ruin that awaits you. Open your eyes and SEE.*

Lightning breeched the sky as I peered through the storm. Beneath the brilliant flash appeared an empty grave. Beside it, lay a mound of dirt and a broken headstone. I squinted through the rain and spotted a deadhead that idled there, on the hallowed ground of section 20.

Section 20... No. Oh, God. No. No...

Surely, you remember section twenty.

Lightning flashed again, revealing the name on the toppled tombstone. But I didn't need to read it. The corpse that hovered mere yards away was that of my father.

Three years, he'd been dead and buried. But in my mind's eye, his cheeks were flush with life. His navy blue blazer hung crisp and straight. His blue checked shirt was clean and pressed, and his striped tie sharply knotted.

A low dark laugh rose through the air, followed by a chorus of cackles that sprang from beneath my feet. The dead were awake — but I hadn't done the waking. Lightning struck again, closer, bathing the sky electric blue and knocking me to the ground. Thunder roared. A tree exploded nearby and burst into flames. By the light of that blaze, I saw my father's corpse had moved.

The sickly smell of decay filled my nose and I knew, without knowing, where he'd gone. Tears welled in my eyes as his moldering hand grabbed my shoulder from behind. I wrenched away sobbing and scrambled to find my footing. Summoning every ounce of strength inside me, I turned to face my father. A sunken mush of brown and black covered his skull, which featured bottomless holes where his eyes had once been. Mummified lips pulled back from his teeth in a hellish grin. His burial clothes hung in tatters, loosely held in place by the rotting waistband of his slacks.

And yet... This monster, this *thing*, was still my father.

Not some nameless, faceless bag of bones. The man who had loved me more than life itself. The man who'd never understood this gift of mine but had sacrificed everything to make sure that *I* would.

Put him down! the brain bitch screamed.

A muted whimpering whirred in my ears. I couldn't place it, but suddenly realized that the sound was coming from me. I fumbled drawing Hawk from my holster. With shaking hands, I swiped tears from my face, leveled Hawk and flipped off the safety.

Oh, Dear God. How can I do this?

How can you not? Little Allie whispered.

Do it, the intruder growled. *You owe me.*

The biter, little more than sinew and bone, shuffled forward, clacking his jaws.

That thing is not your father, Little Allie cried. *Shoot!*

I sobbed and lowered my gun, then stumbled away, with my father snapping at my heels.

Do it! shrieked the brain bitch. *Do it. Now!*

I turned, raised the gun and fired. The *crack* of my 9mm roared above the storm. My father's corpse crumpled to the ground, with me beside him. The wind howled on. And the storm continued to rage, as if the last few minutes could be swept away. As if the torrents could cleanse me of the horrible thing I'd done. The horrible thing the intruder had made me do.

But rain could never scour away this nightmare. Or my anger.

My father hadn't raised himself. I knew who the intruder had been. I knew precisely who had turned my father into a shambling, rotting perversion of the man he had been in life. And I knew why he had done it. The deluded bastard may have thought he was collecting a debt, but I had news for him. I owed him nothing. And paybacks are hell.

"I'm coming for you," I whispered into the storm. "I'm coming."

ACKNOWLEDGMENTS

I would like to express my gratitude to the many people who helped bring this book to life:

Christiana Miller, your drive and focus have given *The Corpse Whisperer* series wings. Thanks for believing in me and Allie Nighthawk.

Robert M. Burdick, who reviewed, suggested, and corrected this manuscript—thanks for giving *Life Among the Tombstones* copious amounts of your time, your literary expertise, and your devotion.

Officer Scott Burdick who has stepped into his father's shoes as my police/weapons expert. You really know your stuff!

And a special shout out to Don Moon and the network of friends and fans who encouraged me. You are too numerous to mention individually, but you know who you are. I will treasure your support and friendship always.

ABOUT THE AUTHOR

H.R. BOLDWOOD, author of the Corpse Whisperer series, and finalist in the 2019 Imadjinn Awards, is a writer of horror and speculative fiction. In another incarnation, Boldwood is a Pushcart Prize nominee and winner of the 2009 Bilbo Award for creative writing by Thomas More College.

Boldwood's characters are often disreputable and not to be trusted. They are kicked to the curb at every conceivable opportunity when some poor unsuspecting publisher welcomes them with open arms. No responsibility is taken by this author for the dastardly and sometimes criminal acts committed by this ragtag group of miscreants.

You can send H.R. Boldwood a message at hrboldwood@gmail.com

To learn more about H.R. Boldwood, visit her website at: www.hrboldwood.com

facebook.com/hrboldwood

x.com/BoldwoodH

bookbub.com/authors/h-r-boldwood

ALSO BY H.R. BOLDWOOD

ALLY NIGHTHAWK NOVELS

The Prodigal

The Corpse Whisperer

Corpse Whisperer Sworn

Corpse Whisperer Torn

ANTHOLOGIES

Killing it Softly (Volume One)

Killing it Softly (Volume Two)

Hyperion and Theia's Saturnalia

Toys in the Attic

Floppy Shoes Apocalypse II

Carnival of Horror

Bete Noire

Pilcrow and Dagger

9 781640 762961